# Ella & Sebastian

Elizabeth Gregurich
& Stacey Hendricks

authorHOUSE®

AuthorHouse™
1663 Liberty Drive
Bloomington, IN 47403
www.authorhouse.com
Phone: 1-800-839-8640

First published by AuthorHouse    9/27/2011

ISBN: 978-1-4490-6155-5 (sc)
ISBN: 978-1-4490-6156-2 (hc)
ISBN: 978-1-4490-6157-9 (e)

Library of Congress Control Number: 2011913956

Printed in the United States of America

Artwork © Stacey Hendricks
Edited by Jennifer Schneider

"The world of reality has its limits; the world of imagination is boundless."

Jean – Jacques Rousseau

# Chapter 1

She was searching for something, or someone, she wasn't quite sure. It was something that felt very comfortable to her, something she may have thoroughly enjoyed at one time, but had since lost and almost forgotten. Like a word that is trapped somewhere deep in your mouth, and it won't come out. Whatever this was that she was chasing through the dark maze was something she desperately wanted, but every time she felt as though she was getting close, the thing escaped her grasp. She couldn't see it, or hear it, but it was something she felt, not with her hands, but with her heart, her soul. And she wanted it now stronger than ever.

She moved more swiftly, determined to find this thing, and she knew she was getting closer, she could feel it. She felt the air move around her, the thing had rounded a corner, just in front of her. She leapt around the corner and scraped at the darkness, attempting with all her might to grab the thing and pull it close and she reached again and knew this was the moment. She stretched her arms out as far as she could, as far as she ever had in her life, and she could almost feel the familiar, comforting thing. It was so close it made her skin prickle with excitement.

# Chapter 2

Rebecca watched the goosebumps rise on her daughter's arms and automatically pulled the starched white blanket up to her thin neck. Appearing to be asleep lay the frail nine-year-old girl, Ella, with tangles of wires stretching from her chest, arm and finger reaching out to the wall.

Rebecca's eyes immediately shifted back to the hospital monitors with the multicolored screen of lines and numbers representing her daughter's heartbeat, blood pressure and oxygen intake. Ella's blood pressure began to drop. One of the anesthesiologists looked at the other and motioned with a finger to stop the slow drip. Dr. Sandt finished the procedure, pulled the 6-inch needle out of Ella's spine and said, "It's done."

Ella, lying rock still, had no idea that her vitals were dropping. But her mother was hyperaware of everything going on. Rebecca's attention never left Ella, her hands never left Ella's frail arm, her mind never left the same prayers she repeatedly recited.

Dr. Sandt looked at Rebecca and smiled a sympathetic yet satisfied smile. She knew what the smile meant. There were only two more treatments. This whole nightmare was coming to an end, finally. Finally.

Rebecca's eyes slid slowly back to the monitors as she watched for the vitals to reach the normal range. She knew that Ella's blood pressure and heartbeat slowed down with anesthesia. That was something she had come to expect with every procedure, but she was still not at ease until everything was back to normal.

Slowly, Ella's heavy, dark lids opened. "Come back," she murmured groggily, still under the influence of the anesthesia.

"I'm right here. How are you feeling?" Rebecca stroked her daughter's short, dark, springing curls. "It's done, Ell. You're all done. And guess what, only two more treatments," Rebecca whispered with a tearful voice. "Only two more." She gripped her daughter's arm a little tighter than usual.

Ella nodded with a hint of a smile and drifted back off for a few more minutes. Rebecca stared at her brave daughter and stroked her face gently.

At the age of six, Ella was diagnosed with Acute Lymphoblastic Leukemia, ALL. It all started with what seemed like a simple cold. Ella proved to be a strong girl and tried to stay in her first grade class even as the cold lingered and worsened to pneumonia. The third round of antibiotics still didn't seem to help. Finally, an ordered blood test had shown the leukemia cells. After that day, the wild ride of chemotherapy began. The past two plus years had been difficult on everyone, but no one could begin to imagine what Ella had gone through.

When they were finally discharged, Ella said her usual thanks to all of the nurses. She could not have survived all of these spinal taps, hospital stays, shots, fevers, and chemotherapy treatments without the support of all of the hospital staff. Expressing herself didn't always come easily, but she always found the words to thank everyone on the fifth floor.

As they walked out of the hospital lobby, Ella stopped for a moment and searched her brain. The feeling of something missing swept over her.

"You okay?" her mom asked a few feet ahead of her.

She nodded. Then, she thought of the next time she'd be back, and just one more time after that. The thought took over her body inside and out and she beamed. Only two more.

She gently grabbed her mother's free hand and they walked out the automatic doors, feeling more hopeful than they'd felt in years.

\* \* \* \*

Ella stared at her blank sheet of notebook paper as she sat at the oak kitchen table. Her thoughts didn't come easily now. She was searching her brain for names as she twirled the curls that sprung off the top of her head with her pencil. Her thoughts quickly moved to her hair and the long wait she had endured for it to grow back. Things like hair and toenails and fingernails she'd never really given much thought to, but after losing them, it was sometimes all she could think about; the mousy brown mop that was too straight to be curly, but too wavy to be straight. She felt really lucky that her hair had come in just as she'd hoped, darker and curlier. She couldn't wait until it grew down her back.

"How's your list coming?" her mom asked, interrupting her thoughts. Rebecca stirred the heaping pot of chicken and noodles that was bubbling on the stove.

"I don't know who to invite," Ella answered.

"Everyone," answered Rebecca matter-of-factly.

"Mom, our house won't hold everyone. Who's everyone anyway?"

"You know," Rebecca walked over to give Ella a huge bear hug from behind. "Everyone that wants to celebrate the end of your treatments. Everyone we know."

"Mom," Ella sighed. Her idea of a fun party was not the house packed with people like a small can of sardines. Ella was more of a one-on-one person. But she knew her mom was right. Everyone would want to celebrate with her, congratulate her and wish her well. Maybe this once she could stand being the center of attention for a house chock full of people.

"And I'll sing a song just for you," a sweet voice chimed in. Ella's older sister, Chelsea, bounced into the kitchen, iPod around her neck. She was willowy with long blonde hair.

"You wouldn't... Please." Ella said with a shake of her head.

"Of course, you're my sister and I love you and I want everyone to know how much," Chelsea said with a brilliant smile. She was almost always smiling. You never quite knew what she was smiling at, but she looked ready to laugh at any moment.

"Well, I think that's a great idea, Chelsea," agreed Rebecca. "As long as it's appropriate."

"Hmm?" Chelsea was playing with a strand of her golden hair.

"Maybe we could get a karaoke machine." Rebecca brightened at the thought of it. "That would be fun."

"Mother, please don't tell me you're going to sing." Ella looked at her with longing, mortified eyes.

"Are you kidding me? Put on some Prince, and watch out!" She began singing "1999" as a little red-headed boy, Miles, came bounding into the kitchen and rushed into Rebecca's thighs. As usual, he was wearing his yellow swimming goggles.

"I want to sing. I want a prince," he demanded. Rebecca swooped him up and started dancing with him.

"Make sure they have 'Somewhere over the Rainbow'," Chelsea sang as she bounded out of the room.

Ella looked mortified. "Chelsea, don't even think of it."

"What? It's perfect. Everyone will cry."

Ella's head collapsed into her arms. "Can't we just go to Disney World or something?"

Rebecca twirled Miles to his place at the table and sat him down in his chair. His spot was marked with multi-colored scribbles of permanent marker, a mishap when Rebecca turned her back. It wasn't smart to turn your back on Miles for more than a minute. He was always into something.

"The idea is to be around the people that love you," said Rebecca as she served Miles his dinner.

"I don't like noodles," Miles said turning up his nose.

"Yes you do," Rebecca reminded him.

"Oh." Miles began slurping down his noodles contentedly.

"Anyway, if we could afford to go to Disney World, I'd take you in a heartbeat. It's just so expensive."

"I know. I was just kidding," she added quickly. Ella knew how much her mother had struggled since her dad died and she was ashamed for even thinking of it, let alone stating it out loud.

"I don't like green beans," Miles piped in.

"Yes, you do," countered Rebecca as she placed the girls' plates at their places at the table. "Chelsea, dinner!"

"Oh." Miles began chowing down on his green beans with a wide grin.

"All right, now let's talk about food. What'll be on the menu?"

"Green beans!" Miles shouted as he spewed green beans across the table in all of his excitement. No one could help but laugh. Even Ella, who was a bit annoyed that her clean piece of paper had just gotten sprayed with green beans, started to giggle at the sight of him.

* * * *

The month passed with more excited party planning. It seemed that everyone in town wanted to be a part of it. Growing up in a small, Midwestern town (population 3,612), just about everyone knew Ella's story. There were many times when Ella just wished they'd lived anonymously in a large city where she didn't have to answer the dreaded question, "How are you feeling, Honey?" There were some days when all she wanted to do was get ice cream with her sister and she would hear this question posed by everyone walking by. But she did have to admit that right now it felt pretty good to have so many people care about her family.

In fact, the guest list was becoming so large, they ended up having to move it to the local Knights of Columbus Hall, who kindly donated it to them free of charge. Ella was actually beginning to get excited about the idea of a big party. Yes, it was overwhelming, but she was finding herself getting swept up in the excitement.

She had decided on a Luau theme. And later that week, after she'd gained some of her energy back from her chemo treatment, she and her mother would shop for leis, coconut-shaped drink cups and grass skirts. The thought of Grandpa Ed in a grass skirt, and she knew he'd be the first to put it on, always made her chuckle out loud. Then she thought of him in public, around everyone, dressed in a grass skirt, and, well, she still laughed. Only two more treatments.

****

"Did you take your medicine, El? Did you?" Miles with yellow goggles in place jumped up and down pulling at Ella's backpack. This had been going on for about 7 minutes straight.

"I told you I did. Now, stop doing that."

"I want to go with you!"

"You're going to preschool and then Grandma's picking you up," Ella stated to him for about the eighth time. Miles continued to jump up and down tugging more harshly at her bag.

Rebecca, quickly pulling on a sweater, rushed up to the bottom of the stairs. "Chelsea, we're going to be late! I've got to get you to school, drop off Miles,-"

"No!" Miles protested, still jumping up and down.

"-drop off papers to my classroom, and then Ella and I have to go to the hospital."

"I'm coming!" Chelsea yelled back. But after several minutes, she didn't come.

"I want to go to the hospital too!" Miles whined as he continued jumping.

"Mom!" Ella urged. She was so ready to get this treatment over.

Miles flopped onto the ground next to Ella's feet, exhausted from jumping.

"Chelsea, now!" Rebecca demanded.

Chelsea came meandering down the stairs with an empty backpack and iPod wrapped around her neck. "I had the greatest dream last night. I just didn't want to wake up," she beamed.

Ella couldn't believe the nerve of her sister. How rude! Making them wait just because she didn't want to wake up from a dream? A dream? A silly dream!

"Where are your books? And you're not supposed to take your iPod to school. Grandma paid a lot of money for that." Rebecca unwrapped the iPod from Chelsea's neck and sent her straight back upstairs. At this point, Miles was kicking the door, hard from his position on the floor.

"Stop! *Mom*," Ella urged.

"Miles, that's enough."

Miles stopped, for a moment. Then, started kicking the door again. "I want to go with you!"

"Chelsea, come on!" Ella yelled after her. Ella knew Chelsea took school for granted, which made her all the angrier, as she stood there waiting again. Ella would have done anything to be a normal student; showing up to class every day, sitting somewhere in the middle to not stand out, and staying quiet unless asked for an answer.

In the last two plus years, Ella had only been able to go to school for half days. Her body could just not take any more. And the half-days weren't frequent. There were large spans of time when she could not go at all whether it was because she was too sick or because the doctors didn't want her to get sick from the other kids because of her weak immune system. At first, missing out on school seemed like it would be fun. But it wasn't. And she just wanted a normal life like every other healthy kid. There was nothing normal about her life since she was six, when she was diagnosed. She could barely remember life without leukemia.

Finally, Chelsea came back down, a few books in her hands. Rebecca grabbed Miles and hurried the kids out the front door.

"Okay, now, Grandma is picking you up, because Ella and I are going to go see the doctor today. Two more treatments, hey, Ell?" She stretched her hand in the air for Ella to give her a high-five. Ella hesitated, looked at Rebecca and touched her hand gently as she got in the van. Miles went in for a very enthusiastic high-five, but missed his mom's hand altogether and somehow landed head-first in the flower bed. After rescuing him from the entangled flowers, Rebecca strapped Miles in his car seat, started the van and looked at Chelsea, who sat in the front seat. "Where are your shoes?"

Chelsea looked at her feet and giggled. "Oh." Sure enough her feet were bare.

Ella collapsed in her seat with a sigh. They were never going to get to the hospital.

An hour and a half later, they did finally reach the hospital. As had been routine for over two years, they stopped at the front desk to sign the papers for their outpatient admittance. Because Ella had nearly become a permanent fixture at St. Vincent's Hospital, Rebecca rarely had to tell anyone what she needed. Without looking away from their personal conversations with Ella, the admitting receptionist brought out the paperwork, slid it all to Rebecca, handed her a pen, took the papers back, and wrapped Ella's tiny wrist with her identification band. It was all that rote.

The hospital workers had come to know and love Ella and her family. Often Rhonda, who had processed Ella's visits more times than Rebecca could remember, walked up to the fifth floor to visit Ella when she had to stay in the hospital longer than one night. She brought pictures to brighten Ella's room and sat for comforting conversations.

Rebecca realized this outpatient visit would be the start of the end of seeing the friends and support people she had met over the last few years. She thanked them for processing Ella's check in, but the intent was so much more. She took Ella's hand, squeezed it, and looked down at her daughter. This was all coming to an end. They both walked a little quicker than usual with that thought.

*****

Chelsea stared at the ticking clock in her second hour language arts class. 10:00. *Ella will be starting her treatment soon,* she thought. After dozens of chemo treatments, 10:00 was never easy. She thought about the last couple of years. How it had affected all of their lives. She shook off the thought of this disease taking her mom away from her when she needed her. *That's selfish,* she thought. Anyway, it was all going to be coming to an end. She knew her mom would now be able to come to her volleyball games, make her lunch, help with her homework, spend time talking about the boys she liked and the girls that were mean to her. As she stared through the clock, she smiled at the thought.

"Chelsea, are you listening?" her teacher asked, annoyed, as she walked up to her desk. "Please. Pay attention."

Chelsea looked up to Mrs. Cameron and smiled politely. "Sorry."

****

Ella sprinted through the darkness, chasing something… someone. She could feel it within her reach. It was warm and comforting. The excitement rushed through her bones. She was so close to finding what she had been missing all of this time. And then it disappeared.

****

Rebecca stroked Ella's hair. She was recovering from the spinal tap and anesthesia beautifully. The procedure had gone so smoothly, it seemed to take no effort or time. Dr. Sandt patted Rebecca's arm as usual and walked out.

With eyes still closed, Ella's lips moved slightly. "Don't go." A single tear slipped down the corner of Ella's dark eye and trailed over her cheekbone. Rebecca smoothed her daughter's cheek. "I'm here. And only one more treatment to go," she whispered, "only one more."

*****

Rebecca sat at her desk making plans for the following weeks. Looking at her classroom, she realized her front bulletin board was the same as it had been all year. She added it to her to do list.

*Change north bulletin board.*

Her list was usually made up of only the essentials. Why would she add to her list something that really seemed so meaningless at this time in her life?

She smiled as she thought about the fact that she might actually get to work on her to do list. She placed her elbows on her desk, rested her head in her hands and sighed. She had made it through this surreal episode, kept her job, and now faced a new beginning. A beginning where she could stay late and grade papers, even take the time to speak with some of her colleagues. She would get to play Power Rangers with Miles and talk to Chelsea about boys. Her world was going to open up soon and she felt as though she were the richest woman in the world.

Rebecca was startled when the door to her classroom creaked open. Expecting to see one of her students or a fellow teacher, Rebecca was taken aback as her mother's face came into focus.

"Mom, what are you doing here? You okay?"

Even her mother's jolly, plump face could not hide the concern. Instantly Rebecca knew that something was wrong. With a frozen voice she begged, "What is it?"

"Dr. Sandt needs to see you right away. Cayce called me to come get you. They didn't tell me anything except that they need to see you."

Instantly, Rebecca knew what they were going to tell her. Ella's cancer was back. But how? Why? She tried to shake it off. No, no, it couldn't be. It just couldn't. But her aching heart told her differently.

Rebecca continuously fired questions at her mother as they drove to the hospital. Judy had no answers to give. She was simply the messenger.

Two constants encompassed the drive to the hospital; hand holding between her and her mother, and the incessant question of, "What are we going to do?" Even with Judy's encouragement to stay positive, Rebecca's mind was filled with the worst possible scenarios.

Rebecca and her mother nearly ran into the hospital. They wanted to hear everything he had to say immediately. As they were escorted into the conference room, Cayce, Dr. Sandt's devoted nurse, stared down at the ground in front of them. As they joined Dr. Sandt at the table, the tears began to well up in all of their eyes. As he began to explain the dreaded news, Rebecca interrupted quickly. "You said this cancer wouldn't come back while she was on chemo. I don't understand. How could it be back while she is still receiving chemo?"

For two and a half hours Dr. Sandt explained that Ella's leukemia had returned, but this time it was in her central nervous system, not her bone morrow. Because they had only been giving Ella chemotherapy treatments in her spine every three months, the leukemia blasts had been able to come back. Ella had relapsed, and she was headed for three more years of more intense chemotherapy and radiation treatments. She listened intently, but all Rebecca could think about was, *How am I going to tell Ella?*

Rebecca sat in the van in front of the house for what seemed like hours repeating that same question. *How am I going to tell Ella? How will I tell all of them?* She didn't know if she could do it. She wasn't sure if she could handle it, let alone her nine-year-old daughter. Judy was in the house now taking care of the kids until Rebecca could get it together. Could she get it together? Just then, Ella knocked on the driver's side window. Lost in her thoughts, Rebecca jumped.

"Are you ready?" Ella asked excitedly.

"What?" Rebecca rolled the window down.

"*Mom.* The party favors, remember? The luau."

A wave of nausea rushed through Rebecca. She looked away from Ella's beaming face and stared at her white knuckles still clenched around the steering wheel. She took a deep, burning breath and stretched her aching fingers.

"Let's go inside." Rebecca quietly crept out of the van and put her arms around the frail girl. She picked her up as she had when her little girl was six and she had carried her to her first chemotherapy appointment. Ella was quiet and laid her head on her mom's shoulder, afraid of what Rebecca was not telling her.

Once in the house, Rebecca set her daughter down on the couch and looked at her deep eyes. She had to just say it. She had to.

"Your leukemia has come back."

Ella stared at her mother with emotionless eyes, limp cheeks, and drawn mouth. She quietly laid her head in her mother's lap. Without a sound, without a movement she laid in the same spot limp and lifeless. This was too much reality for Ella. The girl who thrived on reality, the girl who only trusted reality, the girl who had been through enough of this reality, could not take this much reality. She was in so much disbelief, she could not react.

The room was dead silent. Rebecca began to focus on the silence so much, the room began to spin, as she waited for Ella to speak, to cry, to react in some way.

Finally, Ella began to whisper, "No, no, no. No, no, no." Her words became louder and entangled with shouts and tears.

"Does this mean two and a half more years of treatments? Will I lose my hair? Do you mean I have to start all over again?" She searched for the answers in her mother's eyes, answers her mother did not want to give.

"Yes," her mother finally answered. "I'm so sorry, but yes."

"Why? You said we were almost done. You said I was done with the hard stuff. You lied to me! You said I WAS DONE!!" She threw her head back into her mother's lap and began to sob.

As though given permission, Rebecca began to cry with her. She held her as tightly as she could, trying to squeeze the pain away. It did not work. Ella cried sad, angry and confused tears until she had no more to shed.

Finally, Ella slowly got up and walked up the stairs to her room to be alone. She needed some time to soak this all in.

Judy carefully walked into the room and put her arms around Rebecca who felt like she had been kicked in the stomach. This was the hardest thing she had ever done. Harder than trying to explain it to six-year-old Ella. And now she had to tell Chelsea and Miles. They would have different emotions for their own reasons, but they would all be affected heavily, again. Their lives would be driven by treatments, sicknesses and hospital stays all over again. With no more stalling, Rebecca gathered Chelsea and Miles to tell them the dreaded news.

****

The next day Ella and her mom were sitting with the team of doctors and nurses. Ella begged the doctors for facts, wanting to understand everything. During one of her many jolts awake in the middle of the night, she'd come to the conclusion that there could have been a mistake.

"Are you sure you were looking at my spinal fluid? I mean, is it at all possible that the slides were mixed with someone else's?"

She wanted to predict everything. She wanted the menu of chemotherapy handed to her right then. She needed the itinerary of her life for the next two and a half years. She needed to know every physical ramification. She needed to see her life drawn out for her in black and white.

The doctors could only speculate what was ahead. There were some written-in-stone treatments, but no one could predict how Ella's body would react.

Ella sank into her mother's lap and separated herself from the several pairs of eyes that were staring down on her. She had trusted everyone in this room when they said that she was to be done in one month. They were all wrong. Who could she trust now?

# Chapter 3

Three months had passed since they'd received the news of the relapse. There was no party because there was nothing to celebrate. Ella was back to square one, as though she hadn't just gone through years of hell already. She was to do it all over again and she could not stand the thought of it. She lay in the same hospital bed she'd been staying in on and off for over two years and she would continue to stay in for another two to three years.

The treatments Ella was receiving were even more intense now. At every treatment, she'd have to spend at least four days in the hospital and the powerful chemotherapy made her feel even more sick for several days after leaving the hospital. Her energy level was lower as well. No matter how hard it was on Ella's body, Dr. Sandt insisted she had to have it on schedule. The fact that the relapse happened before she'd reached remission told the doctors that her previous chemotherapy had not been strong enough. The high potency was now causing her hair to come out in clumps, something she'd prayed would not happen again.

She had to give up her horse therapy lessons. This was something she had been doing for the last six months. Ella had always loved horses and her weekly lessons became something she so looked forward to. Rebecca assured her that once she was feeling better, she'd be able to ride again, but Ella wasn't holding her breath. She knew her energy hadn't been high enough for her to do much of anything these days.

* * * *

Two more long months passed and Ella's curly, brown hair, the hair she cherished after the first bout of treatments, had mostly fallen out. Only a few dark patches remained. Her skin was very pale and the dark rings that seemed to be fading at one time, now reappeared darker than before. She looked like a cancer patient.

Ella lay in the hospital bed completely listless. When she felt like this, she couldn't talk, didn't want to talk, couldn't respond, couldn't think, couldn't do anything. She knew how hard this was on her mom, who felt completely helpless. But Ella couldn't try to maker her feel better now. She couldn't put on her happy, brave face. Quite literally, she couldn't do anything.

There was an IV that was attached to the port in her chest. The port had been implanted into the right side of her chest when she was first diagnosed to make it easier to give her medication. The other end of the IV tube was attached to a bag of liquid chemo that hung from a tall pump which was plugged into the wall, releasing just the right amount of medicine. She stared. Drip. Drip. Drip.

Her eyes slowly moved to the small, white light atop the hospital monitor in the corner of the room. She concentrated on the white light as she had done on many occasions, just trying to lose herself and focus on something other than what was going on in that room. It didn't work.

Ella slowly rolled away from the light, her mom and the window to the outside world that just reminded her of what she was missing out on and stared out her hospital room door.

There she could see the nurse's station. She didn't want to see anything or anyone. Luckily, there were no nurses, no smiling faces, no discussing kids or what they were going to make for dinner that night. It was just nothing, which is all Ella could handle at the moment. She was restless yet couldn't really move. She felt nauseous but that wasn't what was making her feel this way. She was just so uncomfortable, so unsettled, so blah. She shifted around, attempting to get somewhat relaxed, but it was no use. She could not, literally, could not, take this any more. She tried to close her eyes, but even that was not comfortable. How was she going to get through two more years of this? She couldn't stand feeling this way one more moment!

That's when she saw him, a strange boy marching through the hall and past her door. And he was marching and singing like he didn't have a care in the world! He'd march one way, then turn around and march the other. What was he doing? Why was he doing it?

Although physically Ella couldn't react, this struck her as very odd, very peculiar, not just because of his marching, or his singing, or even the fact that he looked way too old to be acting this way. This boy really stood out because he had a big mop of black, curly hair sitting on top of his head. Thick, shiny, beautiful, black, curly hair in fact. You didn't see many kids with that much hair on the fifth floor cancer ward of St. Vincent's Children's Hospital. Of course, when children were first diagnosed, they'd come in looking normal. She, herself, had a bronze mane when she first arrived. It was so thick it had broken the ponytail holder on several occasions. She remembered when she first saw other kids on the floor who'd lost their hair. She had pulled at hers to see if it would come out, but it didn't. Not until about three month's worth of chemotherapy. Poor, dumb kid, he had no idea what he was in for in the next few years. How could anyone know how terrible leukemia truly was?

She continued to watch him marching back and forth in front of her door. It completely annoyed her. Didn't he realize there were other patients on the floor? Others with a care in the world. Others who were going through a lot of pain, a lot of worry, a lot of sadness. Why was he so happy?

But she couldn't take her eyes off him. There was something familiar about him, something almost comforting. She didn't understand why she had this feeling. He was completely crazy. It was as though he were leading an entire marching band- complete with loud horns, thundering drums, clanking symbols, the whole lot. She could almost hear the loud, thumping music they made, see the band members marching in their tall red and white hats with tight straps around their chins, gold tassels on their shoulders, big shiny buttons sewn to their finely pressed coats and pants. Cheerleaders with puffy pom-poms. Dogs jumping through hoops. She even had thoughts of an enormous elephant whose head had a giant purple plume sticking out of it. Of course, she couldn't really hear the music or see the parade. That would be impossible. It was just a silly boy in tattered clothes marching through the hallway, who had now disappeared.

\* \* \* \*

Ella lay in her bed and stared at the small TV at the foot of the bed. "Wizard of Oz," a family favorite, played on the DVD. Ella's room was small, but very lively, painted in bright colors of pink and purple with aqua bubbles, an attempt by her family to make the room as cheerful as possible. There were stuffed animals, dolls, board games, puzzles, art supplies, CDs, DVDs, and several books lining the shelves on subjects such as horses, space, Mexican pirates, the Magellan expedition, the ocean and many others. No doubt presents that loved ones thought would keep a homebound girl entertained over the last two and a half years.

There was also a large fish tank next to Ella's bed with two goldfish and one angelfish hiding in the corner. On the bottom of the tank, blue and green pebbles were scattered around fake caves and boulders. In the middle of the tank a "sunken ship" with skull and crossbones painted on the mast, rested on its side, the perfect place for the timid angelfish to hide.

There was a knock on Ella's bedroom door and Chelsea slowly crept in.

"Ell, want some hot chocolate?" she asked. Ella shook her head slightly and continued staring at the TV.

"Do you want anything?" Again, Ella shook her head, not looking at Chelsea. Chelsea was concerned. Ella certainly had had times when she was not feeling well and times when she was sad, but it was different this time. It had been two weeks since she'd been out of the hospital and Ella barely spoke.

"I saw Sarah when I was picking up your homework. She wanted me to tell you 'hi'. She misses you." Chelsea looked for a smile, a reaction of some sort, but there was none. Ella remained silent, staring at the TV.

"Hey, remember when Mom used to do her impression of the lollypop kids?" Chelsea laughed hard. "Oh my gosh. That was so weird." Ella remained mute. Chelsea bit her bottom lip with worry.

She carefully climbed into bed with her sister and laid her head gently next to Ella's on the pillow. Seeing the two sisters side by side, it was obvious that they could not have looked more different and their personalities mirrored that. Chelsea usually had her head in the clouds, daydreaming about the most lovely types of things. Ella, on the other hand, had her head and feet firmly planted on the ground and had been from a very young age. Some speculated that it might have something to do with Ella's age when her father passed away, but Rebecca could see the serious personality in her daughter even as a young baby. She could look into her eyes at that young age and knew there was a lot of contemplation going on in there.

The girls continued to watch the movie in silence.

Rebecca sat at the kitchen table, checking through Ella's homework. Ella was missing a lot of school now, so Rebecca was missing several days as well. But when she absolutely had to be at work, she had a plan set in place. Her older sister, Ann, watched Ella on Mondays, Rebecca's dad had Tuesdays, her younger sister, Laura, took Thursdays and Rebecca's mom had Wednesdays and Fridays. Thank goodness for family and friends Rebecca thought on several hundred occasions. What would she have done without them?

When Ella had to go into the hospital, all of the family pitched in and took turns spending the night with Miles or taking Chelsea in for a few days and shuttling her to and from school and the hospital. Rebecca never left the hospital. She didn't want Ella to be without her for even a moment.

Rebecca watched Chelsea walk into the room. "Chels, get your math book. Mrs. Ryan told me you have a quiz tomorrow."

Chelsea walked up to her and sat on Rebecca's lap. "You okay?" Rebecca asked as she looked straight into her eyes.

"Ella won't even talk to me. It's like she's not even herself anymore."

"I know," Rebecca said sympathetically. "She's going through a really rough time right now."

"I think she's sad and depressed." Chelsea thought for a few moments, then sprang up with an exciting idea. "What if we threw her a party?"

"Well, I'm not really sure she's up for a party."

"Then we should take her on a trip. Get her out of this house. She'd like that."

"She would," Rebecca said not quite sure that Ella would be up for that either.

"She needs to get her mind off things for a while. It seems like it's just too much," Chelsea said thoughtfully.

Chelsea was right. Rebecca didn't know if it would be possible, but there were times when Dr. Sandt could give Ella a blood transfusion to boost her energy. One thing she had learned through all of this is how important it was to give Ella things to look forward to.

Rebecca looked at Chelsea's worried face. "I'll talk to Dr. Sandt tomorrow and see what he thinks. Now, you need to study. I want to hear all good things about your grades when Spring Break comes. Okay?"

"But my show just started."

"Chelsea." Rebecca gave her the look.

"All right." Chelsea reluctantly headed to the living room to retrieve her textbook.

Just as Dorothy and the gang were approaching the wizard's door, Ella turned off the television. She turned over on her side, but unable to get comfortable, she turned to the other side and stared at the fish in the tank. She tapped on the glass very softly because she didn't want to hurt the fish. The two goldfish followed her finger eagerly as she outlined figure eights and then tucked her hand back under her pillow. She watched the angelfish hiding in the sunken ship. The fish's big eye peeked out of the hole in the bow of the boat. Ella watched for a long time before finally closing her tired eyes.

# Chapter 4

Somewhere in the middle of the dark sea, vicious waves crashed against the side of a strong, wooden ship. On deck several mangy-looking pirates with shredded clothes, dreaded hair and scarred faces thrashed their dull swords at one another. Sparks flew, filling the midnight sky with bright orange, blue and green.

Their sword fighting was good, but could not be matched by the handsome pirate with long, curly, dark hair and the body of a twelve-year-old, who appeared out of mid-air. His garb was in mint condition with stark white ruffles, spit-shined paten leather boots, a shiny satin cape, and a velvet hat with a brim wide enough to cover his entire face.

Although lanky, he fought the other pirates off with much strength and finesse. He stunned them with quick strokes and sudden jabs, sending all whom he fought to their knees. The pirates were frightened of this boy. One started to cry just by the sight of him. Another jumped ship. He'd rather deal with the sharks than have to take on the Fearless Pirate.

As the boy defeated the last pirate, he stood with his hand on his hip. "All hail, The King of all Pirates, The Hero of the Seas! He has saved the Island of Goats Smell!"

He easily pulled his dark, wavy hair to the side, revealing his identity. This looked to be the very same boy that was leading the marching band through the halls of the hospital. He stood there, grinning from ear to ear.

\* \* \* \*

*"Dreamcatchers" is a dream-come-to-life for every boy and girl who passes through the hand-carved doors. In 1962 Roger Finnegan built the amusement park by hand realizing that every child deserves to have a place to dream.*

"Hmm." Ella finished reading the sign and looked around the park. It may have been quite something five decades ago, but now it seemed a little eerie to her.

There were several families rushing towards the entrance. Kids of all ages, sizes, and races were jumping around with excitement. Families spoke a variety of different languages. *This place is a melting pot in and of itself,* Ella thought.

Ella sighed. At this stage of her relapse, she was again quite swollen due to her weekly chemotherapy treatments. Dr. Sandt had given the okay for the trip, after giving Ella a blood transfusion, but the rejuvenated feeling was temporary.

Rebecca took Ella by shoulders and asked, "You feeling okay?"

Ella quietly nodded with her gentle smile. Her pale face and dark rings said differently, but she was bound and determined that she was not going to let it spoil their vacation.

They walked through the entrance of the park and past an aging, bronze pirate statue. Just then, Rebecca was dragged through the park by the red-headed tornado, Miles, with goggles firmly in place.

"Let's go over here! Ooo, look, it's a cave!!!!"

Rebecca motioned for the other girls to catch up. Chelsea tried to keep her cool appearance. She was 13 after all and this place was swarming with boys about her age. Ella followed.

They reached a cave with palm trees and ferns hovering over the entrance. The petrified sign read, "Los Piratas de Cozumel."

"Let's go! Let's go!" Miles dashed to the entrance.

"Miles, let's let Ella decide where we start," suggested his mom.

"It's okay," Ella answered quietly.

"Yeah!!! Let's go, let's go, let's go!" He spun wildly like a cartoon Tasmanian devil.

As Ella followed the others into the ride, she took notice at the peeling paint on the cave walls and the wires sticking out of the plastic greenery. Several pieces of ABC gum lined the entryway. The family of four stepped into the wet raft.

"Ah! Look at my skirt!" grimaced Chelsea as she patted her behind.

"Calm down. It will dry," insisted Rebecca.

Ella took the seat in the back.

Instantly, they were all thrown back as the raft bucked into the dark cave and past old, stiff mechanical figures. Some moved very rigidly. Others didn't move at all. The "Mayans".

"Cozumel is Mexico's original Caribbean playground. The Mayans, its first inhabitants, considered it a sacred shrine and referred to it as 'Ah-Cuzamil-Peten', meaning 'Island of the Swallows,'" the woman's voice over the loudspeaker explained.

The raft "floated" past the Mayans and towards a scene of Spanish explorers in a boat viewing this new land through a telescope. A mechanical explorer jerked around suddenly and the telescope nearly sideswiped the raft. They jumped.

"The Spanish first arrived on the island in 1518, early in their conquest of the New World."

The raft bucked towards mechanical pirates and a beat-up old ship.

"Several pirates used Cozumel as a base of operations in the 17th century. The island provided refuge to many including the dreaded Jean Lafitte and Henry Morgan, The King of all Pirates. These pirates sank countless merchant ships, the wrecks of which litter the ocean floor today."

As they began to buck out of sight, Ella's eye was caught by a figure flashing behind the skull and crossbones mast. She looked at the others to see if they had caught it, but no one took notice and Chelsea was too busy ogling the boy in the raft in front of theirs.

Ella peered back and just caught a glimpse of a dark figure as the raft disappeared around the corner before she could get a good look. As she strained her neck, the raft came to a stop and they family of four stepped onto the concrete platform. All of their behinds were soaking wet.

"Let's go again!" exclaimed Miles.

"You said we could go into the gift shop after. It's right here," countered Chelsea.

Rebecca was torn, attempting to keep everyone happy. "Miles, Honey…"

"Ella, don't you want to go again?" Miles lifted his goggles and pleaded with his beautiful, blue marbles for eyes.

"I'll take him," offered Ella.

"I thought you wanted to go shopping," Chelsea said to her.

"We'll be here all week. You go ahead. I'll take him'" Ella said, really wanting to see if she could get a better look at the mystery image.

"No, I don't know," Rebecca said very protectively.

"Mom, please, it's right here," Ella pointed out.

"All right, I'll wait for all of you right here. Right. Here."

They left their separate ways. Rebecca looked in both directions, showing concern all over her face.

Ella and Miles floated by the pirate exhibit where she thought she had seen the figure. Nothing. Just then, the raft jerked to a stop. It was stuck on the conveyer belt. A look of panic covered Miles' face.

Over the loud speaker, they could hear, "#36 stuck in pirates' cove again."

Miles got even more nervous. "Ella, what's wrong?"

"It's fine. We're just stuck. They'll free us in a sec," she assured him. She held him closely. He buried his head in her chest.

In the background, one of the mechanical pirates started moving a little too human-like. The figure jumped out of the exhibit and towards their raft, thrusting the boat free. Then, it disappeared out of sight. It all happened so quickly, Ella didn't get a good look, but just caught a glimpse of the dark silhouette of a boy. Miles screamed bloody murder. She held him more tightly.

"It's okay, Buddy. Here we go." They were on their way.

As the park worker arrived, the boat sailed out of sight. He rolled his eyes. A wasted trip from his comfortable stool at the command center.

Miles wailed as they emerged from the cave. "I never want to go on that ride again. It's too scary."

Chelsea grabbed his hand. "You want to see scary? You should have seen the belly shirt this girl was trying on in the gift shop. Two sizes too small."

"What's a belly shirt?" Miles asked, pretty sure nothing could be as scary as what he'd just experienced.

"You don't want to know. C'mon, Miles, let's go see the boa constrictor." She pointed to a winding, serpentine roller coaster. The dull green cars looked like the body of a snake.

"What's a boa constrictor?" Miles inquired.

"It's a snake that squeezes you to death." She squeezed him tightly.

Miles screamed again. Rebecca hurried to console him. Ella looked back to the cave and wondered about the mysterious boy in the cave.

****

The Lucky Clover Motel was a good compliment to the amusement park; an older motel with just the bare necessities, but it was clean. The room had two double beds with large floral print comforters that Rebecca immediately stripped off the beds. She'd seen the Dateline that revealed all of the bacteria that was on hotel comforters. There was a nightstand, a small television with rabbit ears, and a wooden table with two mismatched chairs. There was also a small lima bean-shaped pool right outside their door.

Miles was sacked out in one of the beds. Chelsea impatiently jumped up and down in her bikini at the door leading out to the pool. "C'mon, Ella, let's go."

"I'm coming." Ella sat at the round table, lining up her extensive medication.

"Come on!"

"Chelsea, I'm coming."

As Rebecca was making one of the beds with her own blankets, she said, "I'll watch from the door. Stay where you can touch."

Chelsea bounded out and gracefully cannon-balled into the pool.

"How many times have I told her not to jump into pools that she's not familiar with?"

"About a hundred," Ella answered back.

Soon, Chelsea was surrounded by three boys about her age. She giggled and tossed her long, golden hair.

Ella sat at the table and, one by one, began swallowing all nine pills lined in a row, largest to smallest. Prevacid for stomach problems. Dexamethasone, a steroid, which was in the form of two pills, 4mg and 1mg. Trexall, her chemo drug. Mercaptupurine, another chemo drug. Colace to keep her regular. Dapsone, an antibiotic to stop any infection that may arise. Diflucan to keep mouth sores down. And, finally, Kytril, another medicine to keep her from getting sick. Ella knew all of these names by heart. And she knew what each did. At age 6, when she began her pill popping, she insisted on knowing. At first, when she would ask what they were for, everyone would simply say, "To make you better." Ella would not accept that and absolutely refused to take any pill until she was told the specifics of how this particular medication was to make her better.

She swallowed down the last pill when Rebecca reminded her, "No food…"

"For an hour, I know," said Ella with her mouth full of water.

Rebecca looked at her with a thoughtful smile, "Of course, you do."

She turned to tuck Miles in whose leg had fallen from the bed. "Oh, and, Ella, put some sun…"

Rebecca turned to find Ella dowsing herself with sunscreen. Rebecca smiled. "You better take it out to your sister."

Ella started out with two towels and the sunscreen. "Bye, Mom."

As Ella headed to the pool, Rebecca's cell phone rang. She watched out the door to her girls as she answered. "Hi, Mom."

"How's everything going?" Judy inquired.

"We're fine. I don't know if this was such a good idea. She won't say anything, but I know she doesn't feel well."

"It's good for her to get out. She's been in that hospital way too long," Judy stated. That was one thing Rebecca always appreciated about her mother, she was always very positive.

"Yeah, but I think this is just too much. She's trying to have a good time, but…"

"Don't worry. You're doing a good thing for her," Judy reassured her.

"I hope so," Rebecca said as she watched Ella, concerned.

Ella sat by the pool dangling her feet in the water and watched Chelsea who was being splashed by the group of boys. They giggled wildly.

* * * *

Miles and Chelsea were sleeping soundly in one bed. Miles swung his arm around, and his hand cupped Chelsea's face like a pale, stubby spider. In the other bed, Rebecca stroked Ella's head, who was on the verge of sleep herself.

"The boys sure do like Chelsea," said Ella.

"They like you too."

Ella shrugged. "That's okay. I'm going to focus on my career."

Rebecca chuckled to herself. "Well, good for you. What career are you focusing on?"

"A nurse, I'm pretty sure. Except I hate puke. Blood I'm okay with but puke, I don't know if I could stand that."

Rebecca smiled to herself. She and Ella had been through plenty of puke spells in the last two and a half years, mainly the result of the chemo.

"Or a hair dresser," Ella said as a second thought.

"I think both are good choices."

"Thanks for bringing us," Ella said with a yawn.

"Well, it's no Disney World. But you... we all deserve a little vacation. You just need to take it easy if it's too much." Ella had fallen asleep in her mother's arms.

Rebecca stared at her beautiful daughter with the big eyes and continued to stroke her head. She remembered the first time she had to explain to Ella that she had leukemia. At the time, it was the most difficult thing she'd ever had to do. How do you tell a six-year-old that they have a very serious disease that will consume their lives for over two years?

Now, though, the entire family had learned to take life one day at a time. Especially Ella, who now just wanted to know where she had to be when and what she had to do next. All she wanted now were the facts. She didn't want any predictions and never discussed when this would all be over. She learned the hard way that there are no guarantees with leukemia. And she was not going to make that mistake again.

# Chapter 5

It was the boy from the hospital again. But this time his black, curly hair was tucked under a beat up old leather pilot's helmet. He turned upside down in his bright yellow and blue spotted airplane. He could hear a plane whizzing by and several rounds of ammunition spraying. The boy then took a nose-dived toward the ground, just missing the enemy plane. It was quite obvious that it was the enemy plane because it was jet black with a skull and cross-bones painted on it and the pilot made evil cackles every time he flew by. He also wore a pencil-thin mustache that accentuated his wickedness.

It seemed that no matter what fancy flying the boy performed (and he did a lot of tricks, spinning, rolling, and twirling), the enemy was still on his tail. Without being able to shake him off, the enemy plane had the boy in his sights and hit the trigger, spraying his plane with ammunition, which wasn't bullets, but something much messier--tomatoes!

The boy quickly veered to the left and swooped underneath the enemy plane. He jetted upward where he was under the black plane and perpendicular to the ground. He hit the trigger and plastered the bottom of the enemy's plane with his tomatoes. The menacing plane swiftly veered to the right, but the boy was in complete control. He leveled the plane with the ground, drifted back just a bit to get a good look at the enemy. He grabbed a big, rotting tomato next to him, pushed a button marked "turbo" and flew full throttle towards the enemy plane. Just as he passed the enemy, he flung the tomato at the man in black. Bull's eye! He hit him directly in the face, spraying rotten tomato all over his flying goggles. The vile enemy couldn't see a thing. Try as he may, he couldn't get the goggles off until it was too late. His plane began sailing towards the ground. The boy watched as the enemy plummeted to the ground and landed in a huge pit of neon green goo. As he sunk lower and lower, the man in black shook his fist toward the boy and slowly disappeared under the slime.

The boy now stood on the wing of the plane as he flew it with his left foot. He took his flying helmet off, his hair blowing in the wind, placed his hand on his hip and grinned widely. He had just saved the town of Kitty Lamb.

* * * *

Miles was wearing his yellow goggles and an enormous smile as he rode the beat-up miniature fire engines around and around and around again. Somehow, the small fire engine made his head look really big. Rebecca snapped photos of him and waved great big every time he came around. The girls waited, sitting on a bench. Chelsea checked a blemish in the mirror of her compact. Ella sat impatiently, looking around at the other kiddy rides. Little tea cups, little horses, little boats, little airplanes, everything slowly going around in circles just like the fire engines Miles was riding. Then she spotted something that really caught her eye. She got up to get a better look and stared intently at the kiddy airplane ride. She squinted a bit and looked again as the airplanes came around a second time. Although she didn't know his name, she certainly believed he looked like the boy with the tuft of curly black hair, marching carelessly through the hospital a few months back. It would have been difficult not to spot him as he was twice as big as the other kids and made jet fighter sounds and looked as if he was dodging enemy fire. What in the world was he doing here?

"Chelsea, look at that kid. He's got to be about your age playing on the kiddy airplanes."

"Hmm?" Chelsea couldn't take her eye off the dreaded blemish.

"Never mind." Ella continued to watch him, completely intrigued by this tween's silly behavior.

As Miles was practically dragged off of the fire engine by Rebecca, he yelled, "I want to ride again!"

Rebecca tried pulling him away from the fire trucks without making too much of a scene. "Miles, it's the girls' turn to go on a ride."

"They can ride too. Pleeeaaaasse!" He began to stomp his foot. A sure sign of a fit to come.

"Lady, is he gettin' off er what?" the older-looking man operating the ride asked. His face was worn and he was hunched over, but his eyes looked much younger.

Ella whined, "*Mom.*"

"Just one more time," Rebecca said. "Go ahead, Miles."

"Then, can we go by ourselves?" Ella popped up off the bench.

"I don't think so."

"Mom, it'll be fine. We could meet at the snow cone cart in a half hour."

"He'll be just a minute and we'll all go together," insisted Rebecca.

"Mom, do you really think he's not going to want to ride again? We all know Miles better than that," Ella said.

Rebecca couldn't argue with that. "A half an hour and don't talk to anyone. I mean, anyone."

She took off her watch and handed it to Chelsea, who for the first time had taken her eyes off the pimple. "What?"

Ella grabbed the watch and Chelsea and headed in the direction of the kiddy planes.

"Be careful," Rebecca pleaded, pretty certain she had made the wrong decision in letting them go.

Ella searched all of the planes as they passed by, but the boy was nowhere to be found.

Chelsea looked at Ella totally surprised. "Please, first I get a pimple the size of the grand canyon and now we're going on the kiddy planes?"

Ella looked around at the other rides, but couldn't see him anywhere. For some reason of which she was not sure, she was completely intrigued by this boy with the hair. She'd just never seen anything like him. He was weird, true, but something pushed her to find him again.

Chelsea, searching for anyone that might see her in the kiddy rides, spotted a massive slide, five stories high across the park. "HEY, let's go on the slide."

"A slide?" Ella questioned, but then she saw it. A gigantic slide, six times the size of any she'd seen in her lifetime and quickly realized that this could be fun.

The girls smiled widely at each other as they hurried over to it and began to climb the steep metal steps to the top, prickly, woven mats slumped over their arms. It was definitely built in the sixties, painted a sixties yellow with rust everywhere, but it looked fun as people were flying down the slide on their mats, laughing and screaming all the way. Half-way up, Ella started breathing heavily and had to stop to catch her breath.

"Are you okay?" asked Chelsea with a concerned look.

Ella leaned on the guarded railing. "Yeah. I'm okay."

"Do you want me to give you a piggy back ride?"

"No, let's go." Some of the color had gone out of Ella's face.

"If you need a rest, just tell me."

"No, come on," and Ella started back up the stairs.

When the girls reached the top, they could see almost the entire park. They spotted Kiddy Land and swore they could hear Miles begging to ride the fire trucks a fifth time.

It was now their turn to place their mats at the top of the slide. The less-than-enthusiastic teen park employee with braces started his memorized speech without a look to them. He was much more interested in the string he was tightly winding around his purple finger. "Keep your hands and feet on the mat at all times. No touching anyone or anything. No rough housing. And no throwing objects of any kind. Go."

The two girls pushed themselves off at the same time. They began gaining more and more speed the further they flew. They were neck and neck. The wavy slide made them sail off their mats, airborne and then landed back on their mats, making their stomachs do summersaults. They giggled uncontrollably. Then, they flew back up and again their stomachs jumped. At this point they were full on belly laughing. The adrenaline was rushing. Chelsea hit the finish line first, and skidded to a halt on the Astroturf. Ella followed soon after and ran smack dab into Chelsea. They flopped around giggling, both trying to get up.

"That was so cool. Let's go again," Chelsea managed to get out between laughs.

"Yeah," Ella agreed. This was the most energetic Ella had felt in a long time and certainly the most fun she'd had.

As she followed Chelsea back up the stairs, she looked down to find the strange boy, the one she'd been looking for, in the "Circus of Games". She noticed him right away, looking very peculiar as the other two times she had seen him. He had an empty box and a stick that he was whipping in the air.

Chelsea was now several steps ahead. She stopped to see that Ella was not right behind her. "You okay?" Chelsea hollered down to her.

Ella started up the stairs but could not help looking back towards the boy, who was now jumping and stretching and making odd "Ya!" noises.

Chelsea yelled down to her, "Are you coming?"

"I'm kind of tired. I'll wait for you down there."

"Are you okay?" Chelsea was worried.

"Fine. I just need a little rest. Go ahead. I'll see you at the bottom."

Chelsea started down the stairs. "I'll rest with you."

"Chelsea, I'm fine. Go ahead. If you were me and I was you, I'd go."

Ella stepped back down the stairs. Chelsea felt very conflicted, but slowly headed up the steps.

When Ella saw Chelsea heading safely up the steps, she walked over to the "Circus of Games" and as she passed one of the games, "Lion Tamer," Ella looked at the suckers throwing their money down. Five dollars for one chance to try and throw a hula hoop around the stuffed lion. The hula hoop never completely landed around any of the lions. *The hoop's oblong*, she thought to herself. *It will never go around. Throwing their money away.*

Her mind was soon empty of the unfairness of the carnival

games when she found the boy only a few feet  behind the Lion Tamer. He was still making his crazy sounds and contorting his body in odd ways, all the while whipping his stick and jabbing his box at the air. Ella stayed just far enough away where she could watch him curiously, but out of his sightline.

*He looks like he is Chelsea's age, but acts like he's a little kid*, she thought to herself. She wondered if something was wrong with him.

The boy, wearing a bright green bowtie and a tux with tails to match, had a huge black top hat sitting on his head, a whip in one hand and a chair in the other. A massive, toothy lion roared into sight. With a quick whip in the air the lion obeyed and took his place on top of a brightly colored pedestal with three other lions and two tigers. The boy strutted around the circus ring, the crowd going wild with applause and cheers. With another quick snap the animals obeyed and reared up on their hind legs. Another gesture from him and they all roared loudly. The crowd grew even louder and stood to show their enthusiasm.

After watching the boy, now in his plain, shabby clothes for a few moments, Ella inched a bit closer. This kid was so into whatever he was doing, he wouldn't even notice her. She was certain it was the boy from the hospital many months ago. He was wearing the same tattered clothes that he wore at the hospital. He still had all his hair. What was the deal with this kid?

"Are you the flying unicorn?" he asked.

This startled Ella. She wasn't quite sure if he was talking to her or not as he was not looking at her and still had the distant look on his face.

"You'd better get to your trapeze. After I put my head in the lion's mouth, you're on."

She stood there, motionless. He inched closer to her. Slowly and carefully, he said, "Don't move." Ella's ringed eyes widened.

He spoke without looking at her. "The saber tooth is right next to you."

She looked around puzzled, and a bit freaked out. Why had she left the big slide to come here? He was crazy!

"Yaaaa!" He snapped his stick in the air with a sharp whip. She jumped. Then, he moved a few feet away from her and continued his taming.

Quietly, she said, "I thought the tiger was over here."

"Can't you see? I'm taming the monkeys," he said as if she had said the dumbest thing he'd ever heard.

Quickly, she started off. "I've got to go."

"Too bad. You'd make a great trapezer."

She stopped for a moment. What in the world was he talking about? She wasn't sure what made her do this, but finally she asked one of the many questions that had been nagging her about this crazy boy.

"How old are you?" she blurted out in a way that really was saying, "You're too old to be acting like this".

The boy didn't seem to get the tone and very matter-of-factly stated, "I'm seven-and-a-half."

*Seven and a half? There's no way he's younger than me*, she thought. Of course, he did act like he was much younger than her, but he was taller than Chelsea. He looked like a teenager. How in the world could he only be seven-and-a-half?

She started off again, but soon her curiosity got the better of her. She turned back to him with an interested look.

"Are you sick too?" she asked.

"I don't think so. I don't have a stomach ache."

"Then, why were you at the hospital?" she asked moving closer to him.

He ignored the question and asked, "Are you gonna be here tomorrow?"

"What do you mean? Here? Like this spot?" She felt herself going a bit hot. "I mean, well, we're going to be at the park again tomorrow. Yeah. How about you?"

"Oh yeah. I'm always here. I live here. See ya tomorrow." He skipped off.

She watched him with an even bigger look of questioning and a bit of annoyance on her face. She shook her head and started towards the big slide. Weird.

Chelsea was nervously biting her nails at the bottom of the slide, looking from person to person. Ella came bounding up to her and took her by the arm. "C'mon. We can't be late. Mom won't let us go by ourselves anymore."

"I was waiting for *you*," Chelsea reminded her as Ella dragged her past the Lion Tamer.

"Hey, let's throw the hoop. I want a stuffed lion."

Ella rolled her eyes and dragged Chelsea toward Kiddy Land.

That night, Chelsea lay spread eagle in bed. She was obviously in a deep sleep by the sounds of her heavy, rhythmic breathing and the little bits of saliva in the corners of her mouth. Ella lay next to her, wide awake. Her head was filled with thoughts of the strange boy.

# Chapter 6

The next morning, Ella and Chelsea were busy whispering in a corner of the hotel room. Miles watched them very carefully and then walked over to his Mom who was packing a lunch for them to take to the park.

"Mom, Chelsea and Ella are whispering," Miles tattled. "And they won't whisper to me."

"I tell you what," Rebecca said as she crouched down to Miles' level and whispered in his ear.

Miles started laughing quite loudly. "Good one, Mom! You're a good whisperer." He looked over his shoulder at the two girls who had not heard any of their conversation and were still deep in conversation. He laughed loudly all the way into the bathroom and continued to laugh as he closed the bathroom door for all to hear. Rebecca smiled to herself as she continued to pack the grapes into the bag.

"You two about ready?" she asked the girls.

They quieted down instantly and carefully made their way over to their mom.

"Mom," Chelsea started.

Ella elbowed her in the ribs and said under her breath, "Not like that. Like we practiced."

"I mean, *Mom*," she started in an over-the-top sweet voice that would have given anyone a toothache. "We were wondering if we-"

Ella elbowed her again and gave her the "remember what we talked about" eyes.

"Oh, yeah, you look really nice today," Chelsea remembered.

"Thanks," Rebecca said suspiciously.

"Well, we were thinking, besides how pretty you look, that since we were so good going on our own yesterday. We didn't talk to anybody."

Ella intentionally did not respond to this statement.

"Not even the cute boy that said 'hi' to me and I'm sure he now thinks I'm stuck up, which I'm totally not-"

"We wanted to go by ourselves today," Ella interrupted too pained to hear any more of Chelsea's commentary.

"Yeah," Chelsea agreed.

"Girls, the park isn't a place where two girls should go by themselves. I'm sorry, you're just too young."

"Mom, Chelsea is almost 14," Ella argued.

"In eight months," Rebecca countered. "I'm sorry, girls. A half an hour is one thing. All day. I just don't think…"

"Well, maybe if you would have bought me the cell phone like I asked for. All my friends have one."

"A 13-year-old does not need a cell phone, Chelsea."

"Fine!" Chelsea threw herself on the bed and planted her head in the pillows.

"Okay, Mom, I understand," said Ella very rationally. "What if we went by ourselves for two hours? That would be okay, wouldn't it? And we'll even stay in the same part of the park. I promise."

Rebecca thought about this for a moment. She sighed, debating the urge to protect her daughters at all times and giving them a bit of space. Maybe an emergency cell phone wouldn't have been such a bad idea.

"Well, one hour and you'll tell me exactly where you're going. If it works out, maybe we'll try it again tomorrow."

"Mom!" Miles yelled from the bathroom. They looked over to find water oozing from underneath the door.

"Oh, no. Coming, Miles!" Rebecca sprinted to the bathroom.

"Looks like we're going to have to work on her a little more," Ella said to Chelsea.

"Should I start crying? I'm really good at it."

"No, I think we need to prove to her that you are responsible. It's gonna be hard, but we'll think of something."

Chelsea scrunched her face, thinking. "Hmm. That will be tough."

****

"Okay, so we've got exactly fifty-seven minutes. This line is too long." Ella complained as she and Chelsea stood in the back of the line of the Boa Constrictor roller coaster where the line snaked around for what looked like miles. "I'm going to get a drink," she said as she spotted a concession stand nearby.

"All right but come right back. People don't like it when you try to save spots."

Ella waited to order her soda. There was no line, but the park worker was gabbing away on her cell phone, apparently oblivious to the fact that she had a customer.

"No, she did not!" the girl said aghast.

Ella had very little patience for this sort of thing and as she expressed her annoyance by throwing her head back with a sigh, spotted the strange boy skipping by the concession area. She stuffed her money back in her pocket and followed him. As usual, he was in his own little world. She cautiously approached him. When he saw her, it was as if she'd been there the whole time.

"I like your head," he stated to her as he slowed his skipping to a playful walk.

*What a strange thing to say,* Ella thought and uncomfortably smoothed down the little hair that she had left. "It fell out."

"I bet it doesn't get in your eyes." He blew his long, black wisps to the side. They immediately fell back over his dark eye. "And it looks cool."

Ella caught herself in a spontaneous smile for a moment and blushed with a look down at her shoes.

"You know, I've seen you before," she finally said to him.

"Yeah, yesterday."

"No, before then. At the hospital."

"I don't know," he said shrugging his shoulders.

What doesn't he know? He was either there or he wasn't. But she knew she'd seen him there and decided not to press the issue for now. Maybe he did have a mental problem.

"Where do you live for real?" Ella asked.

"All over, but mostly in Pirate's Cove."

Ella smirked. "No one lives in an amusement park."

"Uh huh. I do." And he said it so earnestly that Ella really thought he believed it. *But no one lives in an amusement park*, she reassured herself.

"Yeah, right," she said, making sure he knew that he couldn't pull one over on her. "Where do your mom and dad live, the funny house?"

"No. Up there with the birds and the clouds."

"Oh," this took Ella aback. "You mean? Sorry."

The boy shrugged.

"Well, someone has to take care of you," she insisted.

"My grandpa did, but he fell over and didn't get back up. I'm not sure, but I think he's up there with the birds too," the boy responded with little emotion on the subject.

Ella looked at him questioningly. "You mean heaven? My dad passed too..." she trailed off. "But how did you end up here?"

"Me and my grandpa came here and rode some rides and he fell over and the security guards came and then the sirens came and took him. And I stayed here."

"But that can't be. They wouldn't just let a kid stay by themselves. Adults won't let you. I mean, my mom won't even let me go by myself for more than an hour," Ella proclaimed.

The boy shrugged again disinterested in the topic. But Ella was very interested and her wheels were turning. "Unless they didn't know you were with him. Didn't someone try to find you? Didn't they miss you?"

He ignored her last question. "Come on, the race is about to start." He darted in the direction of the carousel.

"What? That's for little kids." But the boy, who was getting stranger by the moment, had already mounted one of the vibrantly colored horses, dancing on its back hooves.

Remembering that she left Chelsea, Ella hurried back to the Boa Constrictor. Chelsea had made very little headway as the rollercoaster had gotten stuck midway through. The kids on the ride didn't seem to mind as they cheered raucously. Chelsea was giggling at three boys about her age. They were doing all of the talking as she had promised her mother she wouldn't speak to anyone. She giggled some more.

Ella rushed up to her, out of breath, "I'm going on the carousel." She hurried back toward the carousel.

"What am I supposed to do?" Chelsea yelled to her.

"Come on!"

"The carousel," Chelsea said sarcastically so the boys could hear, but her bright face revealed that really she liked the idea of riding the carousel and she ducked under the railing. She smiled back to the boys who looked disappointed that she was leaving. And she headed for Ella. "Wait for me!"

By the time Chelsea reached the carousel, it was too late. The carousel operator had closed the gate.

"Halfta wait 'til next round," he said in a thick southern accent. She plopped down on a bench next to the ride.

Ella mounted a horse behind the boy. *This is stupid*, she thought to herself. *He must be crazy.*

The festive music started as the horses slowly began sliding up and down. *Here we go,* she thought. *Around and around and around.*

The strange boy didn't find it boring. She looked at him hunched down in a racing position, kicking the horse to go faster. *Oh yeah, he's nuts*, she thought to herself.

Chelsea waved at Ella who rolled her eyes to relay, "What was I thinking?" back to Chelsea.

Ella looked back to the boy in his shabby clothing who was really getting into it.

Now the boy was in full jockey's uniform, bright pink with a big, red number 9 on his back, matching the blinders of his horse, a real horse. A sleek brown filly with a blonde mane and tail. The horse raced down the track with the boy on her back. Other racehorses and their riders, surrounded him, but his horse sped up with a "giddy-up!" and they began passing the other horses with no problem. He looked behind him. "Come on, Ella!"

"How do you know my name?" Ella yelled up to him. She saw him in reality, on his carousel horse in his normal frayed clothes, but it was as if he was riding a real racehorse and he was looking at her as though she was in the race as well. She looked down at her horse just to make sure she wasn't missing anything. It was just a plain old, fiberglass carousel horse like everyone else was riding.

When the boy looked back to her again, she was in jockey uniform of yellow with an aqua number seven on her back, riding a beautiful silver stallion. And she was gaining ground. He whipped his horse to go faster and laughed excitedly, "Yoo-hoo!"

Ella gained more ground and passed two other horses. She was making her way up to the boy and his horse. They were neck and neck, riding side by side. The excitement was written all over his face. He could see the finish line 50 feet away.

In Ella's reality, the carousel horse slid up and down to the festive music. Boring.

Still neck and neck, the boy looked over at Ella and smiled. Ella looked at him strangely. Just as they crossed the finish line, his horse just nosed ahead. The winner!

The carousel slowly came to a halt. Several kids clamored to get off the ride at once, obstructing Ella's view of the strange boy. Ella stepped off the ride and strained her neck to look for him. He was nowhere to be found. She headed for Chelsea. "Did you see that kid in front of me?"

"Oh, the little boy with the blonde hair. Wasn't he cute?"

"No, not him." She strained her head to look over the crowd, but he had disappeared. She finally gave up. "Come on. We'd better go meet Mom and Miles for lunch."

"Ah. I didn't get to ride one ride," Chelsea complained.

"Once we're done with Mom, we'll be riding all day by ourselves. Don't worry," Ella assured her.

The girls set off to meet Rebecca and Miles. They arrived at Kiddy Land and spotted Rebecca standing by watching Miles on the fire engines, of course. They ran up to her breathlessly.

"We're here, Mom."

"Yeah, with 10 minutes to spare," Ella grabbed Chelsea's arm wearing her mother's watch.

"You were right, Chelsea," Ella said. "It was good that we didn't ride again. We would have been late."

"Huh?" Chelsea was not catching on.

Ella elbowed her as Rebecca waved to Miles. "Remember, I begged you to ride one more time, but you insisted that we meet mom and not be late? You were right and very responsible, right, Mom?"

"Yes, yes." Rebecca smiled, knowing exactly what they were up to. She handed the girls her backpack and said, "Why don't you go get us a table? You can start on lunch. Miles is almost done."

Miles chugged around in the fire engine beaming at them.

The girls took their mom's bag and picked the sun-faded salmon-colored picnic table nearby with initials carved all over it. Ella began taking the turkey sandwiches out of the bag, followed by grapes, pretzels, and water bottles.

Chelsea let out an annoyed gasp. "Again? Why can't we just eat the food court food like normal people?" She pointed to the extremely long line of impatient, agitated customers waiting to give their greasy, overpriced orders at the concession window.

"Chelsea, it's really expensive to eat here. You know Mom doesn't have money for that. Heck, she really didn't even have money to bring us here, but somehow she managed it. You should be a little more appreciative."

Chelsea looked away, ashamed.

"Okay, now, we have to figure out our plan to make Mom think you're really responsible. You need to help her out as much as possible. You know, help her with Miles. Help her with lunches, stuff like that. And it might help if you brought up conversations that adults talk about."

"Like what?"

"You know, ask her about her day, talk about current events." She noticed Chelsea's blank look. "Things you'd read in the newspaper or see on the news."

The light bulb went off. "Oh."

Just then Miles came bounding up to the girls. "Oh, you should go on the fire engines. They are so much fun. The last two times I went, the siren was broken, but that's okay." He spotted the sandwiches. "Mmm, lunch!" Miles grabbed the other half of Chelsea's sandwich and a fist full of pretzels.

"Hey," Chelsea argued, but then saw her mom coming and said loud enough to make sure her mother could hear, "That's it, you go ahead and eat all of my sandwiches that you want. And if you want more, I'll make them for you. But Mom's are the best. No one could make a better sandwich than Mom, but I'll try." She smiled, very proudly as she patted Miles on his head.

Rebecca looked at her questioningly. Ella shook her head.

\* \* \* \*

On the car ride back to the hotel, Ella sat in the front of the van with her mom. Chelsea sat in back with a sacked out Miles looking through an old newspaper. She put it down and cleared her throat. "So, mom, what do you think of this global warming thing?"

Rebecca looked at her in the rear view mirror very surprised. "Uhh, well, I think it's scary. And we need to take responsibility and do something about it. Why? What do you think?"

"Oh, yeah. I think that children are our future and we need to do something about it."

Ella looked back to Chelsea in disbelief. Chelsea proudly gave her thumbs up.

"Well, it seems like you two had a good day. Very responsible." said Rebecca.

Ella looked back at Chelsea and they both beamed at one another. Just what they were hoping for.

"Ella, I want you to rest for an hour before going swimming, okay?"

"Why?"

"If you want to go back to the park tomorrow, you need some rest."

"Mom, I'll help you with dinner while Ella is resting," said Chelsea, helpfully.

Rebecca looked at her in the rear view mirror with a very surprised look on her face. Even Ella, who had put Chelsea up to this, was taken aback.

"Wow, Chels, I'd really appreciate that," Rebecca said. She thought for a moment, then added, "Maybe we could talk about you two going by yourselves a bit longer tomorrow."

Chelsea sat up straight and smiled, proudly.

The van pulled into the motel's parking lot. Chelsea jumped

out and started unbuckling Miles from his car seat before Rebecca could get to him.

"I've got him," Chelsea said straining to carry the sleeping boy to their room.

"You sure?" her mom asked as Chelsea staggered towards room #103.

Ella looked at her mom. "Told ya. You just need to let her be responsible."

And then Chelsea fell into a bush and Miles landed on top of her with a thud.

# Chapter 7

The next morning the family hit the park as soon as it opened. It helped that Chelsea got dressed without having to be reminded several times and she also helped get Miles dressed and the lunches made. Rebecca was amazed and told the girls that they could go by themselves that morning and they would all meet up at the gift shop later that day. She was still a bit concerned, but she was impressed enough with Chelsea that she thought she owed it to the girls. After all, they were really trying hard.

"All right," she said before sending them off, "the same rules apply. No talking to anyone. Always stay with each other even when you go into the bathroom. I want you in the same stall. Never, ever leave each other's sight. Hear me?"

The girls, delighted about their freedom, nodded simultaneously. Miles held his mom's hand impatiently jumping up and down, anxious to get to the rides.

"Okay, I'm proud of both of you. Now, be careful. If anyone or anything is suspicious, go straight to a policeman. Don't go to security. Those are just a bunch of drop-outs. Oh, and, Ella, you need to drink lots of water. And-" the girls looked at her warily, "have fun."

"Let's go to the fire engines!" Miles exclaimed as he pulled his goggles down over his eyes and grabbed his mother. Rebecca watched the girls as he pulled her out of sight.

The girls quickly headed to the roller coaster thinking it was early enough that they had beat the rush and there would not be such a long line. They were right. There were only about 20 people in front of them. As they anxiously waited for their turn, they watched the snake serpentine on the tall tracks. Their hearts raced as the roller coaster plunged from about 4 stories high. This was going to be fun.

A group of three girls in front of Chelsea must have felt the same way because two of the girls were giggling wildly. The third, younger girl looked completely freaked out. She had bright red hair and freckles covering her face. She looked a lot like one of the older girls, but younger.

"Please, go with me, Jordan," the redhead pleaded.

"I'm going with Melissa," responded her sister. "You'll be fine."

The redhead looked back at Chelsea. "You don't need a partner, do you?"

Chelsea, not wanting to break her vow of silence, shook her head, holding back any words.

Ella spoke up, "Sorry, she's my sister. We're going together."

"See, Jordan, she's going with her sister."

"Chelsea, you can talk to her," Ella said knowingly.

"Mom said-"

"I don't think she meant scared little girls."

As the next group got on the roller coaster, the girls moved in even closer, now under the enclosure where they could see the cars being loaded. Ella and Chelsea's hearts raced even faster.

Finally, the little redhead looked incredibly panicked. "I can't go by myself, Jordan."

"You have to. I already told Melissa I'd ride with her. If you'd brought a friend with you-"

The little girl gasped with fright, her eyes huge.

"Poor girl," said Chelsea to Ella.

"I know. I wouldn't want to go by myself either."

Just then, Ella spotted the strange boy waiting in the line by himself, a few people behind her. She thought for a moment and then said to Chelsea, "You go with her. I found someone to go with."

"Who? We're not supposed to. Are you sure?"

"Yeah, it's fine. I'll meet you down at the bottom." Ella started back towards the boy.

"Okay, if you're sure," Chelsea said very unsure. She strained her neck to see who Ella was going with, but the little redhead overheard Ella and jumped up and down, tightly hugging Chelsea with relief.

"Thank you, thank you, thank you."

Chelsea lost sight of her sister which concerned her very much.

Ella reached the boy, with excitement shooting out of her. "Hi, do you have a partner?"

"No, I always go by myself," he answered, not at all surprised to see her.

She wasn't sure if this meant he wanted to go by himself. "You want to ride together?"

"Only if we can ride in the very back. It's the best."

"Well, you would know," she said.

As the rollercoaster came to a sudden halt and the passengers got out, Chelsea and the redhead boarded the very first car. A few moments later, on their turn, Ella and the boy hurried into the last car.

Ella waved to Chelsea, but Chelsea couldn't see her over the large headrests. As she watched them, Ella wondered if it wasn't such a good idea for Chelsea and the redhead to be taking the first car since the little girl looked a bit green with fright. She then looked over to the boy and asked, "What's your name?"

"Sebastian. You should know that," he answered. He was making gestures as though he were a monkey.

Ella wasn't sure what he meant when he said that she should know that, but then again she wasn't ever quite sure what to make of him. At this moment, she was a bit embarrassed to be seen with this boy who was so peculiar and acting as though he were a monkey, but then the cars started to move and her attention turned to the ride. She was so nervous, excited, and full of anticipation, she didn't really care what the strange boy was doing.

The coaster started its ascent up the clanking conveyer belt. They reached so high, they could see most of the park. As they inched higher and higher, the rickety, old roller coaster seemed as though it were going to give out and send them shooting down backwards. But as Ella saw the first car with Chelsea inside plunging over the hill, she knew they would soon follow. Chelsea and the redhead screamed on the top of their lungs as their car was the first to begin plummeting down the hill. Ella's heart raced even faster and quickly she looked over to Sebastian whose arms were now in the air, but he still had a strange monkey-look on his face.

Just then, Ella and Sebastian were jerked in the same direction as the preceding cars and they began plummeting. Ella got an uncontrollable case of the giggles and held on for dear life. As they reached the bottom and the cars jerked back up and around, her stomach dropped. Now, she could hear herself screaming along with everyone else. Everyone except for Sebastian who although was enjoying himself did not look like he knew he was riding a roller coaster. He looked like he was somewhere else.

The coaster sent them up and down around and then back up and over and every way imaginable. After the biggest hill of all, the cars jerked to a stop and slowly crept into the tunnel where they knew the ride was over. *Too short*, Ella thought with a big smile on her face. Her little wisps of hair stuck straight up.

All of the passengers got off at the same time, so Ella couldn't see Chelsea, but she was sure she had as much fun as Ella. She wished she had gone with Chelsea now, because Sebastian was still in his little world, flailing his arms, not conscious of the fact that the ride was over.

Ella waited for a moment for Sebastian to get out of the car like the other kids, but he still sat there, making his monkey movements. She looked around, embarrassed, but no one seemed to be paying him any attention.

"We have to get off," she said to him with a little nudge.

"Wow, I love going to the Amazone!" he yelled as he got out of the car.

As Ella followed Sebastian and the rest of the crowd through the winding maze of the exit, she asked, "What were you doing up there?"

"Riding the boa constrictor, of course."

It didn't look like he was just riding a roller coaster to her.

"Come on, we'd better get our boat." Sebastian pointed to the entrance of the log ride.

"Oh, I have to go find my sister."

"All right, but hurry. Pale face is coming," warned Sebastian.

Ella automatically touched her translucent cheek as she watched him go. Then, she spotted Chelsea waiting at the bottom. Chelsea had a sick look on her face.

"Didn't you like it?" asked Ella.

"Yeah, until that girl puked on me."

"Oh, gross." At a closer inspection, she did have chunks of vomit speckled all over her leg.

"I'm going to go to the bathroom to wash it off. Come on, I can't stand the smell one more minute."

Ella looked back to the log ride entrance where Sebastian was waiting for her. "Can you go by yourself? I want to go on the log ride."

"Mom said we couldn't let each other out of our sight and that we had to go into the stall together."

"I'm not going into the stall with you. And, look, there isn't even a line." She pointed back to the entrance of the log ride where Sebastian was in an odd, squatting position, arms out like he was pulling back a bow. "I'll meet you right back here in ten minutes."

"Oh, all right. But don't tell Mom."

"Don't worry. We worked too hard for this."

Ella raced back to Sebastian and they hurried up to the hollowed out plastic logs that he referred to as boats.

"Goin' by yourself?" the park worker asked Ella.

"No, he's coming too."

The park worker shrugged. Sebastian enthusiastically boarded in front and Ella got in behind him. He instantly began making a rowing motion. They floated along the pathway and through the tall, green, fake trees. Wild animal sounds (Ella noticed the speakers mounted in the trees) could be heard echoing through the ride. Ella continued to watch Sebastian, mesmerized by his playing. He was very watchful of his surroundings and looked as though he spotted something in the trees other than the speakers. He stood up and gracefully drew his arm back again and with a snap, it was as if an arrow shot out of a bow. *It really looked like it,* thought Ella.

"Got it!" he exclaimed. "We only kill what we need. We eat the meat. The fur will make warm blankets in the winter, the bones we can use for more arrowheads and the teeth will make a nice necklace."

"The hooves could be used to grind corn," Ella chimed in trying to play along.

Sebastian looked back to her and nodded his head with a smile. She smiled to herself.

Two Indians slowly floated down the river in a hand-carved canoe through the forest.

As the boat arrived at the dock, Ella looked at Sebastian intently. She thought for a moment and then carefully stated something that had been on her mind ever since she laid eyes on this boy. "You know, you look like you're my sister's age, but you act like you're younger than me."

"I bet a lot of kids act younger than you." As the boat stopped on the bumpers, Sebastian hurried out. "See ya!" He raced out of sight, very much like a gazelle, leaving Ella wondering.

As she appeared out of the exit, Chelsea walked up to her. "I swear, I can still smell it. Ooo." She scrunched her nose up in disgust.

Ella grabbed Chelsea's arm, very carefully. "Come on." She pulled her in the direction of the gift shop.

The girls met Rebecca, and Miles at the gift shop. Chelsea

looked for anything fashionable that would get the smelly clothes off her. Ella eyed a cool leopard print top and tried it on. She admired it in the mirror with a big smile. As she walked out to show her mom, she spotted Sebastian kicking rocks up in the air outside of the large storefront window. Ella looked at her top. The price tag showed a big $28. She looked at Sebastian again with his raggedy clothes, pants too short.

Rebecca walked up to Ella and admired the top. "Oh, that is so cute on you."

"Yeah, I don't really like it." Ella turned up her nose.

"Are you kidding? It looks adorable on you."

"Nah. I'm gonna look at some pants," she said as she went to take the top off. When she exited the dressing room, she noticed that Rebecca was preoccupied with Miles who wanted everything in the store. Ella browsed the boys section and found a pair of khaki pants for $25. She decided he must be about 13 years old, Chelsea's age, because of his size. So he must be a size 13. She picked up the pants and held them up to the window where Sebastian continued to kick rocks. She sized them up. They looked like they would work.

Ella took them over to her mom and tried to discreetly show them to her. "I want these."

"Ella, are you sure? What size are those?" She looked at the tag, "You don't wear a 13."

Ella gave her that look of "don't embarrass me."

"The 10s hurt my stomach," she said. "They're too tight."

"Okay. If you're sure, but aren't they boys?" Rebecca questioned again.

"Mom, they fit." Ella hurried up to the cash register.

Chelsea approached her mom spotting what was going on.

"Looks like she and I are going to have a little heart to heart about style." She gave her mom a twisted look.

Rebecca shook her head and grabbed the top that Chelsea had picked up and took it up to the register with Ella's pants and purchased them. As soon as Rebecca and Chelsea were distracted by Miles, Ella ran outside to give Sebastian the pants she'd bought for him.

"Take these. I hope they fit," she said taking the pants out of the bag and shoving them towards him as she watched for her mom through the window.

"What's this?" Sebastian asked as he unfolded the khakis. "Wow, these are awesome. Safari pants! These'll be perfect to save the baby baboon from the leopard."

"Yeah, sure," Ella said, "I gotta go before they see me. See you tomorrow?"

"You bet!" exclaimed Sebastian as he admired the pants while skipping away.

Ella hurriedly filled the bag with rocks to make it look as though the contents were still inside. As she hurried back inside the shop, she looked back toward Sebastian who was celebrating by throwing the pants high in the air and catching them with a dive. Ella shook her head. She'd never seen someone so excited about a pair of brown pants.

Miles bounded up to Ella with Elvis sunglasses on complete with the side burns, an extra large Styrofoam cowboy hat with twinkling lights and a bright pink fringed shirt three sizes too big with the printing "Dreamcatchers, where dreams have come true since 1964".

"I want these," he said hopefully.

Ella, Chelsea, Rebecca looked at him and laughter poured out.

* * * *

The Mortimer's went back to their motel room where Chelsea had been helping her mom with dinner.

"Mom, is there anything else I can do?" asked Chelsea as she came back into the room after taking the garbage out.

Rebecca looked at her and smiled. "No, Chels, you've been a huge help, I really appreciate it. Why don't you have some fun with Ella and Miles?"

Miles was sitting on the toilet where Ella was applying blue eye shadow to his eyelids. "I'm not squirming at all, am I Ella?" Miles asked proudly.

"If you want your eyes done right, you can't talk." Miles tightened his mouth closed, almost bursting.

"I'll do a good job. Won't I, Ella?" he asked hopefully.

"If you let me do your makeup right," she warned. He nodded and she gave him a disapproving look for moving.

Ella's makeup had already been applied quite carefully with thick eye pencil around her eyes and quite a bit of blush on her cheeks. A bright pink lipstick accentuated her mouth. Although Ella wasn't one to play make believe, she really had to admit that she enjoyed performing dance numbers with her sister.

Chelsea knocked on the door to the bathroom and went inside, incredibly thankful that she could join her siblings in the fun that they'd planned for that night. "Oh my gosh. I thought I was going to die. I don't know how much more of this being responsible I can take." Chelsea made the quote marks with her fingers when she said "responsible."

"Shh, Mom'll hear you," warned Ella. "You have to just keep playing along."

"Playing what?" Miles inquired. "I want to play."

"Miles, honey, you are playing with us. You even get to be the person in front," Ella said very motherly. He beamed with pride.

"Why do you think we're letting…" Ella said to Chelsea as she gestured towards Miles whose eyes were closed waiting for his mascara. "Now, get ready."

Several minutes later, after Rebecca had made their lunches for the following day and put all of the food away, the girls instructed her to sit in the chair at the table.

Within a few minutes, the girls came out of the bathroom in full costume and make up. They were wearing their bikini tops and towels as skirts. Chelsea's hair was teased out wide and Ella had sprinkled quite a bit of glitter onto her head. Their makeup was bright and thick.

Chelsea strutted excitedly and Ella had a very serious look on her face as she started the music. A funky bass started and soon the song revealed itself to be "Give up the Funk" by Parliament. One of the few of Rebecca's CDs that the girls actually enjoyed.

The girls started their groovy dancing, very close to being in sink. Soon enough, they started singing along with the high-pitched voices, "You've got a real type of thing going down, gettin' down. There's a whole lot of rhythm going round." They twirled and abruptly stopped with their arms directed to the bathroom door when the chorus began, "Ow, we want the funk," where Miles was obviously supposed to make his entrance, but he missed his cue and Ella said sternly under her breath, "Miles!"

"Oh!" Miles yelled back excitedly.

He made his grand entrance, every bit as dramatic as Chelsea's, but with a big grin on his face. He was wearing one of the girls' sun dresses, along with full make-up and a bright pink wig that Chelsea had bought at the gift shop. He looked absolutely hilarious and Rebecca could not hold back her laugh. He took his place in front of the girls and began singing quite loudly, "Give up the funk, Ow, we need the funk, We gotta have that funk." He swung his hips wide, launching himself onto the bed. He bounced off and landed into Ella who pushed him back in his place.

Rebecca could not contain herself. She laughed and clapped loudly.

During the funky musical interlude, Miles was supposed to be in unison with the girls, but during a turn, Miles kept turning around and around (obviously forgetting what he was supposed to be doing) until the point of being completely dizzy and fell to the ground with an uproarious, uncontrollable giggle. Rebecca and Chelsea laughed at the sight and Ella, who had been a little annoyed that he had made several mishaps, was now giggling and collapsed onto the bed.

After praising them for a great show, Rebecca asked them to get ready for bed. Miles, who was up way past his bedtime, had fallen asleep in one bed, with makeup and sundress still on. The girls hurried into their pajamas and their bed, still giggling.

"Okay, time to sleep if you want to go to the park tomorrow."

The girls were face-to-face trying to hold back their giggles, burying their faces in their pillows. They finally closed their eyes to look as though they were attempting to follow their mother's orders.

As Rebecca turned off the lights and crawled into bed next to a snoring Miles, she whispered over to the girls, "I think you've earned the right to go by yourselves for most of the day tomorrow."

The girls, still facing one another, grinned proudly at each other and lightly hit hands in a high-five. Their plan had worked just as they had hoped.

# Chapter 8

The next morning the girls were all over the park, only asked to check in at lunch and then again in the afternoon to reassure Rebecca that they were okay and Ella's energy was holding up. She didn't need to worry about that right now as Ella's adrenaline was running fast and she and Chelsea were having a great time. They even persuaded their mom that she didn't need a hundred more photos of Miles on the fire engine ride in Kiddy Land, so she loaned them her camera, and they were able to capture much of their fun. Chelsea griped about the fact that her mom only had an old film camera and they couldn't look at the photos instantly. But only for a moment because they were having so much fun things like that didn't seem to matter.

They rode the slide about eight times, the Boa Constructor two times (but would have ridden it several other times if it weren't for the long line), the log ride, the white water raft where they got completely drenched, another roller coaster called "The Vibrating Monkey" which didn't make a bit of sense to Ella, the whirl-a-whip that spun them so quickly around Ella thought she might just puke, the swings, and the shooting star that shot them out of sky back to the ground, making their stomachs end up in their throats. Ella had considered going into the observatory, but it was closed and there was a large sign stating that renovations were taking place. So, they rode the swinging pirate ship instead.

They were just about to decide on their final ride before meeting their mom at Kiddy Land when Ella spotted Sebastian doing handstands near the entrance. He was waving his legs crazily in the air.

As Ella watched him, Chelsea suggested they ride the carousel since she wasn't able to get on the first time Ella rode it.

"Why don't you go ahead? I already rode it and there's someone I want to go see."

"Who?" asked Chelsea inquisitively.

"No one. Just go ahead and we'll meet back here in a half an hour."

"Ella, why won't you let me meet your friend?"

"It's no big deal." Ella was lying. It was a big deal to her. There was something about Sebastian that she really enjoyed. Something about being with him that for a short time made her forget she was sick and would be going back into the hospital next week. She didn't know why he affected her this way, but it was really one of the few things that allowed her to not focus on her illness for once. And she knew how boys reacted when they saw Chelsea. She didn't want anything to distract Sebastian from their fun. She didn't want to share Sebastian with anyone.

Ella didn't give Chelsea much of a choice and yelled, "See ya!" as she headed off in the opposite direction of Sebastian, trying to throw Chelsea off. Resigned to the fact that she wouldn't change Ella's mind, Chelsea walked in the direction of the carousel.

When Ella saw the coast was clear, she snuck back over to Sebastian and sat down in the grass next to him. As usual, he acted as though she had been there with him all day.

"Do you know any tricks?" he asked her as he pulled his hands out from under his body and fell to the ground on his head. It was as though he'd done this intentionally and he obviously wasn't hurt in any way.

Ella shook her head. "My sister knows how to do a walkover. She's in gymnastics."

"No, do YOU know any tricks?" he asked more plainly.

Ella shook her head again and reinforced it with a final, "No."

"Do this," and Sebastian did a summer salt, landing spread eagle on the ground. Ella looked around sure that people must be staring at them, but to her surprise no one seemed to think it was strange that this teenage boy was acting in this way. When she looked at him again, he was flopping on the ground.

"What are you doing?" she asked half-thinking he might be having some sort of convulsion.

"Flopping."

"I mean, why are you doing it?" she asked more pronounced.

"Cuz it feels good. Try it."

"No way." She was not going to look as dumb as he, even though astonishingly people still were not looking at them.

"Well, do something. It's no fun to just sit there."

Although it was entertaining to sit there and watch him, he was right. It wasn't a lot of fun to just sit. She'd done plenty of sitting, laying, waiting in the two plus years. So, she popped up but smiled, embarrassed. "I don't know what to do."

"Want me to teach you how to do a somersault?"

"No, I learned that when I was three." She thought for just a moment. "I guess there's something I kind of know how to do."

Sebastian sat up straight, excitedly anticipating her trick. He still flailed his arms around.

67

"Well, okay." She got into her stance, arms straight in the air, right leg out. But then at a second, insecure thought, she turned back to him. "Just remember, I could only take gymnastics 'til I was six, so I was just learning this."

He motioned with a nod to tell her to get on with it. She got back into her stance, breathed in some courage and did her leg curled, lop sided cartwheel, landing on her behind. Her face instantly turned red and she took a moment to look up. It didn't matter so much to her that people were now staring at them, but she was certain Sebastian would make fun or at least feel sorry for her for looking so stupid.

"Cool!" he exclaimed and rocketed out of his sitting position. He did a cartwheel just as she had, legs bent and totally lopsided. He landed on the ground right next to her, a wide grin on his face. "That was super cool." Ella smiled back at him and they darted back up and did the Ella-style cartwheel over and over and over until they were both so dizzy, they landed on the ground and were laughing uncontrollably.

Ella caught site of her mother's watch which showed that she and Chelsea had seven minutes to get back to Kiddy Land. She hurriedly popped up. "I've got to go meet my mom."

"But I wanted to show you something," said Sebastian disappointedly.

"Maybe I can talk my mom into letting us come back after dinner. How 'bout I meet you at six?"

"Well, I don't know what time it is, but I'll just go there and wait for you. Meet me in Aqua World at the big, blue round building."

"Okay," said Ella a bit unsure if she'd be able to talk her mom into letting them go out again. "See you then."

As she started off, she thought how she wished she could

capture this moment and relive it again and again. Then, she remembered her mom's camera in her pocket. "Sebastian, come here a minute."

Sebastian skipped over to her as she walked up to a man nearby who was waiting for his child to get his snow cone.

"Excuse me. Could you take our picture?"

"Your picture? Oh, sure," he said with a peculiar smile.

Ella and Sebastian stood side by side. He stood with his hands on his hips, feet spread apart slightly, wide grin on his face. At the last moment, Ella put her arm around him. Something she wouldn't normally do, but she felt as if she'd known this boy for a long time. They had some sort of connection even though she couldn't imagine what it might be.

"Say cheese," and the man clicked the photo. "I think you'll like this one. You looked great," he said as he handed her the camera.

Ella wished her mom had a digital camera so she could see the photo right away and make sure she didn't look too dumb. She couldn't wait to see the photo of the two of them. She would treasure the photo, capturing a moment of pure fun.

Ella looked at Sebastian and smiled, "See ya at six." She was now bound and determined she would talk her mom into letting them go back out after dinner. She hurried off to the carousel.

Sprinting through the park as to not be late, the girls slowed their pace as they approached the fire engines.

A familiar voice echoed through their ears. "I'm not hungry!" Jumping up and down, beating on his chest with his flailing arms, Miles begged, "Mom, please, oh please let me ride one more thing. I'll never ask again. I'll eat everything on my plate. I'll never ask you to do anything for me again. Please let me ride one…." Mile's head, attention, and dialogue quickly changed directions as he saw his sisters approaching.

"Hey, Ell! Hey, Chels! You can't believe what I did. Guess, just guess!"

"I don't know Miles," sighed Ella, too tired to fake enthusiasm.

"I said guess, come on guess, come on guess," Miles was not going to let this guessing game go. The girls knew the drill with their brother, the annoying game of you have to make at least thirty guesses before he would tell you what he wanted you to know. His tireless nature made it impossible to dodge this one-sided, never-ending, three-year-old enjoyment.

Chelsea played along, as she always did, rattling off numerous impossible suggestions sending Miles into wild laughter. Ella sat down slowly on the bench, showing signs of fatigue. Carefully, she observed her mother gathering her belongings, making sure she disguised all of the evidences of weariness. As soon as her mother looked her way, Ella picked up her shoulders, deepened her voice, and smiled with delight. It worked.

"Girls, you must be having a good time too," she smiled at Ella's shining face. "Let's go have some dinner, get some energy built back up and talk about what we want to do next."

Miles took this as his cue to throw out his ideas. As he uttered his tenth suggestion for after-dinner plans (three of them being ride the fire engines), they walked in the direction of the picnic area. They reached their destination where in the middle stood a massive fountain of a Native American man shooting an arrow from a bow. The plaque read, "Geronimo". The fountain was no longer working and obviously hadn't been for quite some time as the stale, thick water attested to.

There were five dirty ducks swimming around in the green

algae and Miles was bound and determined that he was going to catch one like he had at the Lucky Ducky game where he won a squirt gun for picking a rubber duck with a number four on the bottom of it. He pulled his goggles down and positioned them over his eyes, ready to dive in after them. Rebecca grabbed him in mid-jump and encouraged him to play with the pigeons that were casing the area for scraps. Miles ran after a group that was pecking away at a discarded box of popcorn. They scattered after he frantically chased after them.

The girls found a patch of grass amongst the dirt where Miles was still in view and sat down under a tree for their dinner of more turkey sandwiches, grapes, and pretzels. Just then, Rebecca's phone rang.

"Oh, I'm sorry. I totally forgot to pre-register Ella for next week's hospital stay."

*Why is she so nice to those people?* Ella thought to herself with a disgusted look. Her heart, mind and shoulders sank with her mother's conversation. She had actually had a few hours without the thought of doctors, without the worry of chemo effects, without the apprehension of a hospital stay. She was brought back to reality as her mother recited all of the pre-registration lingo Ella had heard time and time again. "Yes, the same insurance... no changes...yes that's her social security number... yes it's the same billing address...yes this is inpatient. She'll be in for about a week. Okay, thanks we'll be there on Monday."

Rebecca's eyes met Ella's as she closed her phone. "Now Ella, you knew we had this stay coming up, right? Please don't let this ruin your trip."

How could that call not ruin her trip? She was only buying time by being here. No matter what, the sun would set each night and come up every morning, moving her closer to Monday. This time next week she'd be in that same old hospital bed, as far away from the fun and excitement she'd experienced this week as could possibly be. Ella's ears began to ring. Her thoughts froze. She gazed slowly around the park and saw people moving and laughing, but she could hear nothing but that annoying ringing. Her mind swarmed with the reality of it all and felt the exhaustion overwhelm her. No, she couldn't let this bring her down and ruin her trip. She was going to turn her mind off and enjoy her last moments here.

Just as she put on a big smile and mustered up some energy to sound as though she were full of energy, Rebecca placed her hand gently on Ella's forehead and said, "You feeling all right?" She'd been reading the signs for two and a half years and was now very good at it out of necessity since Ella rarely complained. Ella knew it was going to be difficult to fool her.

"Yeah, I feel great!" she said a little too enthusiastically. It didn't help that she was very pale and clammy.

"I think you need to rest. You've been running for four days straight."

"No, no, I'm fine. I'm great!" Ella responded with as much excitement as she could produce.

Rebecca looked at the girls with a sober look on her face. "I think we may need to consider that this should be our last day at the park."

"NOOOO!" the girls whined in unison.

"I know, I know," Rebecca said quickly. "But we need to remember why we came here. To make us all feel better, and we will not leave here with Ella feeling worse."

"Uhh-" gasped Ella.

"Ella, I know we've all enjoyed this trip. And I know this has been really good for you mentally, but we also have to consider the physical. And you know you have limitations."

Ella crossed her arms in defiance, a scowl on her face. She couldn't look at her mom. She knew this wasn't a very mature way to handle the situation, but right now, she didn't care.

Chelsea was silent, looking as though she was carefully considering what her mother had just said. She finally broke the silence.

"Mom, there's going to be fireworks tomorrow night. Could we just rest during the day and then come see the fireworks?" Chelsea asked very thoughtfully.

Rebecca was impressed by Chelsea's rationale. "Well, I was thinking we might go home tomorrow-"

"No!" objected Ella. "This is the most fun I've had—we've had—in a really long time. You can't take this away from us. It's not fair."

"If you would have let me finish," she placed her hand gently over Ella's arms. "I was going to say that I was thinking we'd go home, but you've both been really good and really helpful and Chelsea has come up with a very good compromise. So, I think that's what we should do."

"I still want to come to the park!" Ella sternly said. This was very uncharacteristic of her normal calm demeanor and her attitude took Rebecca, Chelsea, and even Ella aback. She couldn't help it. She wanted to spend the last days with Sebastian as much as possible. She was finally having fun. She had actually forgotten for a moment that she was sick. He was the only one who didn't constantly remind her that she had leukemia. He didn't care. Heck, he didn't seem to even know. He liked her hair, he liked her cartwheels. She did not want to give up a moment of it. She just could not let her mom stop her. She couldn't.

"I think we need to go back to the motel," Rebecca said as she started packing up the leftover dinner. She eyed Miles who was now the one being chased by a herd of pigeons.

"Come on, Miles! We're going back to the motel."

Chelsea was watching Ella, but when Ella remained in the same disapproving posture, she got up to help her mom with the packing. Ella was planning her strategy. She knew if she continued to act as she was, her mother would certainly insist that they go back to the motel and she would have to rest. So, she had to figure out how she could be more rational to get what she wanted--to see Sebastian again. Sebastian was going to be waiting for her at six, and if she didn't meet up with him, he might be mad at her and not want to spend any time with her tomorrow. She finally decided she was going to be honest with her mom. Sort of.

She got up, a much softer look on her face, and walked over to her mom who was throwing out the trash into a garbage can.

"Mom, I'm sorry," she said very honestly. Rebecca smiled gently at her. "I've just been having so much fun. And there have even been times that I've forgotten that I'm sick. I just don't want it to end."

Rebecca grabbed her up and hugged her hard. "I know. But you know it's my job to look after you and do whatever is best for you. I'm not letting anything happen to you." She kissed her on the head and gently placed her back on the ground. They started back to Chelsea who was airing out the blanket and Miles, who was now lying on the ground next to her in a mound of dirt.

"Mom, I'll rest tomorrow before the fireworks. I promise. But do you think me and Chelsea could go out a little bit longer?" Ella saw the questioning look on her mother's face. "I really am feeling a lot better since I ate," she added.

"We need to get Miles back. He is going to crash hard and no one wants that."

"I know," said Ella disappointedly.

When they reached Miles, they found him fast asleep, curled up in the dirt. Rebecca had to shoo the dirty pigeons away from him.

"Chelsea, were you going to let the pigeons eat him?"

"Oh, sorry, I didn't see him there," she said with a giggle.

"Look, Mom, this way Miles could have a nap. We don't want to disturb him, do we? No one wants that," said Ella.

Rebecca sighed and looked down at the sacked out little red-head. "All right. One hour, but you have to take it easy. Hear me?"

Ella jumped up and down and hugged Chelsea. Chelsea looked at her, a little shocked at her excitement.

"Easy," Rebecca quietly yelled at them as the girls headed off to the rides. She tried to pick Miles up, but he made a nasty noise, so she thought it better to leave him there and cover him up with the blanket. She sat down next to him, shooing the pesky pigeons away.

After Ella persuaded Chelsea that she was going to the bathroom by herself and Chelsea could stay and watch the diving exhibition, Ella bee-lined to the round, blue building that had yellow tape strung across the entrance with big black letters stating, "Do Not Cross." She was now feeling completely exhausted and thought maybe she should have taken her mom's advice. She gulped down some of the water left in her water bottle, hoping it would regenerate her. Sebastian soon came around the corner and ducked under the tape, expecting her to follow.

"I don't know," she said hesitantly.

"Come on. I come in here all the time."

She reluctantly ducked under the tape. "I don't have much time."

"Don't worry. It won't take long. You won't want to miss it, though," he said excitedly as he disappeared through the dark gap in the padlocked door. Ella slipped through the gap close behind him.

As they walked into the dark building, Ella could feel a cold chill with a shiver. She couldn't see a thing, but felt the presence of something massive. Was it the enormity of the open space or something else lingering in the shadows? She didn't know and wasn't sure that she wanted to find out.

"I don't think we should be here."

"It's okay." Sebastian took her by the hand and led her further into the black hole. He planted her next to a wall of some sort. "Stay right here."

By this point Ella's exhaustion wouldn't even allow her to respond. The trip was catching up to her. She felt as though she wanted to collapse on the ground and just lie there for days. She leaned on the cool wall heavily, resting her head on the side. She closed her eyes. It was very quiet except for the sound of water swaying to and fro. And she swore she heard a bit of a gentle splash. The sounds of the ocean, whether imagined or real, soothed her, relaxed her. But an ocean? How? She opened her eyes for a moment in disbelief, but was soon caught up in the soothing waves and closed them once again. If she was dreaming, that was fine with her.

Instantly, lights were flashed on, illuminating a gigantic glass tank from under the water. Ella opened her eyes to witness this unbelievable site, glorious blue water shining brightly and projecting onto her pale face. She stared at the empty tank and stroked the glass that separated her and the cool water.

Sebastian appeared out of the darkness. He walked straight for the tank without saying a word. As he neared the tank, he reached his hand out to touch the glass, but instead of being stopped by the hard glass, the glass became liquefied at his touch and his hand penetrated the water.

Ella's heart pounded. How could this possibly be? She blinked several times, pretty sure she was having some sort of hallucination. But the image didn't go away. She was confused, anxious, but totally infatuated. Sebastian slowly delved further in, one body part at a time; hand, arm, torso, leg. He looked over to her with his big smile and within an instant his entire body vanished into the liquid.

"Sebastian!" Ella could not see him, only millions of tiny bubbles. And then, they settled and she could only see the still aqua water. She must have been seeing things. She must have been dreaming. But what a beautiful dream. With closed eyes, she gently rested her head on the glass again soaking in the coolness of the tank's outer wall.

All was again quiet and still. Her breathing became very rhythmic and steady. As her eyes remained closed, a large blue nose inched towards her from inside the tank. It gently poked and nudged at the glass where her face lay. It now had come into full view and revealed itself to be an enormous blue whale who appeared from out of nowhere inside the tank. The whale quietly nudged at her face, almost caressing it. With eyes still closed, Ella instinctively nudged back. At this point she was in a dream-like state and felt so calmed. She didn't dare open her eyes, as she didn't want to wake up and lose this peaceful feeling.

She reached her hand out toward this beautiful mammal,

unaware of what she was reaching for. She reached even further, and this time the hardness of the glass did not stop her, liquefying just as it had with Sebastian. Slowly, her petite hand penetrated the water and soon made contact with the soft skin of the giant. The whale leaned into her touch just as a dog would do when rubbing its ears. He tried to cup his massive head in her tiny hand and faintly Ella could hear a squeal, a beautiful, delightful high-pitched tune.

With eyes still closed, Ella rolled her forehead towards the glass. Slowly, steadily, her fuzzy head pushed its way through the expandable glass and into the water. There they were, a small, frail little girl, head to head with an enormously strong blue whale. They were now not in a tank, but under the sea. Algae floated by, vibrant schools of fish swam between the two. Electrified yellow and orange coral jetted from the ground.

Ella slowly opened her eyes to see the whale's small, glistening eye staring back at her. Startled, she jerked back and gulped in water. She started to panic, frightened she was going to lose her breath. But as she looked at the whale, who hadn't moved and seemed to look at her adoringly, she calmed and soon realized that she could breathe under the water effortlessly.

Quietly, she brought her small hand back to the whale's enormous chin and began to stroke it. The whale started to squeal again, not unlike a high pitched purr. Ella stared into the small black eye and caught sight of the glint in his eye. She looked deeper and deeper, a small white dot that became bigger and took the shape of the white light on her hospital monitor. In the reflection of his eye, she could now clearly make out her sterile hospital room with the monitor next to her bed, the chair her mother always sat in, the small bathroom, and the door out to the nurses' station.

Instantly, she was taken out of her hospital room and brought back to the water as she could no longer breathe and choked in the liquid. The whale, still looking at her lovingly, slowly backed away, out of sight. Ella quickly pulled her head out of the water, choking, coughing up a few tablespoons of the salt water. As the coughs subsided, she pulled back from the tank. She had no idea what had just happened to her. Yes, she did. She had come face to face with a blue whale. That's what happened. But that was completely impossible. It was a dream. Of course, it was a dream. Right?

Sebastian's long hair flowed in the wind and he yelled "Yahoo!!!" as he plummeted into the ocean on the back of a huge blue whale.

# Chapter 9

Ella awoke the next morning in her bed with a broad smile on her face.

"Well, look at you. You must have gotten some good sleep last night. Your coloring looks great," gushed Rebecca. Ella did look refreshed.

Ella sighed with a stretch, "Good dream."

"Dream?" Rebecca knew that Ella had always thought dreams were a waste of time. She smiled as she smoothed the back of her hand along Ella's forehead. "Must have been." She got up and looked at Miles. "Come on, Miles, you need a bath."

"No, I don't," he assured her with dirt still stuck in his outstretched ears. Rebecca swooped him up and carried him into the bathroom with her.

Chelsea hurried over to Ella's bed as Rebecca disappeared into the bathroom. "I still can't believe you just ditched me last night. You scared me to death."

"Oh, Chelsea," Ella said brushing her sister's concerns off.

Chelsea teared up a little. "You said you were just going to the bathroom and you'd be right back. Don't do that. I thought somebody took you."

"Chelsea, no one is going to take me. Okay, I'm sorry. I am. I won't do it again." Dramatically, Chelsea grabbed her in her arms.

"Chelsea. Calm down," Ella gasped through her sister's tight squeeze.

As Chelsea let go, she added, "And I still don't understand how you got all wet."

Ella's eyes widen. What did happen last night? Ella couldn't explain it to herself, let alone to Chelsea.

"I was just sweaty," she said weakly as she started changing into her swimsuit. "Can you believe we can't go to the park today, our last day?" she asked, changing the subject.

"I know. I tried to talk Mom into it, but she still thinks you need to rest."

"I feel great!" Ella exclaimed as she jumped onto the bed.

Just then, Rebecca came out of the bathroom with Miles who was dripping wet from his bath. He ran onto the bed and started jumping with Ella.

"Mom," Ella said in between jumps, "could you…get the pho…tos developed?"

"As soon as we get home," Rebecca answered, tackling Miles to put his Power Rangers undies on him.

"I saw a…convenience store across…the highway. We can get them…developed there. Please."

"Why do you need them so badly?"

"Mom." She gave the "don't ask any questions" look.

"All right. I guess as long as they can have them ready before we leave. And, by the way, we're leaving early to get home at a decent hour. So, no asking if we can go to the park one more day."

All three of the kids whined, "Uhh!" at the same time.

"We had an entire week here. It has to end at some point,"

Rebecca said as she made the bed that Ella and Miles weren't jumping on.

"You're absolutely right," Chelsea chimed in with a big grin on her face. She then winked at Ella.

"A lot of good it does now," Ella whispered back to her. "Let's go swimming!"

The kids headed for the door just as Rebecca stopped them. "Wait, wait, wait! Ella, you need to take your medication. And no one has even eaten breakfast. Of course you'll have to wait the 30 minutes and then you can go swimming." The kids always made fun of Rebecca for the 30 minute rule, but she swore she'd seen kids puke jumping in a pool a minute too soon.

Ella grabbed the bottles of medication off the sink and started popping them one-by-one. "I just felt so good, I forgot about my medicine for a second."

"You must, because I don't think I've had to remind you of that once. Ever." Rebecca smiled at the thought that Ella felt so good she actually forgot about her medications for a moment. The truth was, Ella was also a bit distracted with last night's events. And the thought of how she would spend her last evening with Sebastian. Of course, she'd have to convince her mom once again to let them go on their own. And then she'd have to ditch Chelsea one more time, but she'd get over it eventually. She absolutely had to see Sebastian.

The family spent the morning at the pool that day. They were all together and, believe it or not, they didn't fight once. Rebecca assumed it was due to the fact that they all knew this would be their last day of vacation and they wanted to make it as fun as possible. Of course, there were gripes when she insisted they all rest before going back to the park that night. But eventually, they all fell asleep.

Ella got out of bed as the others still slept and walked out the motel room door. Miraculously, Sebastian was waiting for her on the other side which led directly to the amusement park. For some reason, it did not occur to her that this was strange.

Sebastian took her hand and they walked into the grand entrance of a medieval castle.

A knight with sparkling armor trotted his large horse over the drawbridge. He ducked as he led the horse into the dark castle illuminated by glowing torches lining a wide hallway. The horse then clopped down the long corridor and into an enormous circular stone arena.

The knight lightly pulled back on the reigns to bring his horse to a halt and then lifted his visor to expose his identity. The dark eyes of Sebastian peered out with a wisp of black, curly hair escaping from the helmet. His eye was caught by another figure in armor on the opposite side of the arena. Sebastian smiled, flipped his shining visor back down and got in the ready position. He held his staff high in the air for the other knight to see. In return, the second knight nodded slightly and with a kick to each horse, they were off, horses sprinting full force, directly at one another.

The hooves of the horses pounded the dirt. They closed in on each other with every fraction of a second. Their nostrils flared as each anticipated the arrival of the other.

The knights raised their staffs towards each another and as they crossed one another, their staffs were brought together, creating a magnificent spark of warm light that shot into the dark sky and brightened the entire arena.

As the knights continued to ride past one another, they were illuminated by the bright light which showed the colorful paintings on the stone walls. The light illuminated bright images of brilliant green dragons, multi-colored peacocks, shimmering koi fish, and silhouettes of beautiful silver stallions. At a closer look, the arena was filled with lush greenery; grape vines whose grapes were five times the size as normal grapes, peach and plum trees that spread out so wide, they could shade three Cadillacs, and a flowing creek that rushed to a waterfall that miraculously ran up rather than down.

The knights slowed the horses and turned in unison towards one another. Sebastian's horse came to a slow walk and he lifted his visor to get a good look at the other knight. The other knight had stopped her horse and sat high on the glistening, black horse.

Sebastian's red horse trotted up to the knight. He stopped, peering at the knight.

"Glad to see ya," Sebastian suddenly said with a great smile.

The knight lifted the visor and exposed the big, bright eyes of Ella. She took her helmet off and smiled back at him.

"That was cool." She looked down at her horse and her smile faded a bit.

"I...I just wish I had my horse." With that, Ella's horse changed from the black stallion into her gorgeous silver horse with the black mane.

"Let's go jump the stream," Sebastian suggested. Ella smiled at him as her eye was caught by something in the sky. It was the glowing ball of light that she and Sebastian had created with their staffs. As she watched curiously, the light got smaller and smaller and nearer and nearer. She blinked hard, not able to take her eyes off it. But when she opened her big eyes with the dark eyelashes, the light that she and Sebastian had made, turned into the small, blinking light on her hospital monitor. She looked around and saw her hospital room just the way it always was, sterile and clean. She blinked again and again and as she did, the hospital room became more and more clear. Then, she heard faint yells from somewhere far away.

"Come back! Come back!"

But it was too late. Everything had vanished, even the hospital room. Then, she was back at the motel, lying next to Chelsea.

After a good meal, the girls persuaded Rebecca to let them go to the park a bit early to ride some rides before the fireworks. With Ella's energy seemingly at an all-time high and their last night of vacation, she gave in. She agreed to let them go on their own and they would meet at their picnic spot before the fireworks began and before it got dark. This gave them a little over an hour.

Ella was still feeling quite good. Her spirits were even heightened when she spotted Sebastian on the other side of the shooting star, the ride she and Chelsea had just enjoyed.

"Sebastian!" Ella yelled across a crowd of teenagers and she waved very enthusiastically. Sebastian waved back and motioned for her to join him on his next adventure.

"Is that your friend?" Chelsea asked, craning her neck to get a peek at this mystery friend but still not catching sight of him.

"Yeah. Look, Chelsea, I know I said I wouldn't leave you again, but this is our last day and I'll probably never see him again."

"Well, he can come with us. I don't mind," offered Chelsea, still trying to catch a glimpse of the mystery boy.

"I just don't think you'd really like him."

"Have I ever met someone I didn't like?" The answer to that was simple. Chelsea really did like everyone. In fact, she loved people in general. Ella definitely didn't want to hurt Chelsea's feelings, but she just didn't want to share Sebastian on their last night.

Chelsea saw the look on Ella's face. "Go ahead. Just make sure you are back here in one hour. We have to meet Mom and Miles before the fireworks start."

Ella gave her a quick hug and ran to meet Sebastian who Chelsea could still not locate in the large crowd. "And, please, be careful!" she yelled, unsure if Ella had even heard her.

Chelsea left to take a turn on the Ferris wheel that stood next to the Shooting Star, but looked back towards Ella with a lot of concern.

Ella followed Sebastian into the Star Gazer Observatory. Unlike the aquarium, there was no yellow tape, just a sign posted outside the door that stated there was construction going on in the observatory through the fall of 2005, just a few years off schedule.

Sebastian had obviously been here several times because he easily entered through a back door. Once inside the dimly lit building, Ella thought there was no way they'd be done with construction until 2015 at the earliest, but she concluded that they must have given up on the renovations. There was still much of the equipment lying around; hammers, ladders, plastic sheets hanging from scaffolding, paint buckets, brushes.

With Sebastian's coaxing, Ella followed as he climbed the tall scaffolding. She was a bit frightened, especially when she looked down to the ground and they were a good two stories high.

"It's okay. Come on," Sebastian urged as he was now about three stories in the sky.

As they climbed higher, Ella looked straight up to keep her eyes from wandering to the ground. But this proved to be making her dizzy as well, so she just kept her eyes on her hands as they grabbed the metal bars. Left, right, left, right.

As she reached Sebastian at the top of the scaffolding, she looked up to find the dark "sky" filled with stars as far as the eye could see. There were large, round planets with swirls of vibrant red, blue, yellow, green.

"Wow!" Ella was enamored with the beautiful midnight sky. It was as if she could touch it, but she knew if she reached up, her hand would simply swipe mid-air. Just as she was thinking this, Sebastian reached his hand up towards the glowing universe. "You can't touch it," Ella told him.

Not paying any attention to her, Sebastian stretched as high as he possibly could on his tiptoes. "I wish we could go higher," she said.

With that Sebastian was lifted up off the scaffolding and slowly started to float towards the glowing planets. Ella could not believe her eyes, but there he was, right in front of her, being lifted off the ground. "I'll see you in space," he pronounced excitedly as he was lifted a few feet in the air and climbing higher.

"Don't leave me!" Ella said urgently, but he was still being lifted up higher. She hurried over to him and pleaded again, "Sebastian, please don't leave me."

He shrugged to her and inching out of reach, she hurriedly grabbed his ankles and hung on for dear life, desperately wanting to go with him. She held on as tightly as she could for as long as she could. For a moment it looked as if she would be lifted off into space with him, but she wasn't strong enough and soon her grasp gave way.

"Please, Sebastian. Please come back. I want to go with you."

"Meet me on Juniper!" he hollered back. He was getting smaller and smaller by the minute.

"I can't. I don't know where it is. I don't know how." Her frustration brought tears. "Please, please, come back." But he had vanished into space.

All was quiet. Lonely and quiet. If only she could go with him.

If only she was able to do what he could do. She wanted to. She needed to. Why couldn't she? She decided she needed to get hold of herself. She looked up at the fake stars and planets. Then, she peered down at the ground below. They had climbed up really high. Climbing down would have been even scarier. Resigned to the fact that all she could do was wait for Sebastian to come back, she sat down cross-legged and sighed.

Ella was frustrated with herself for not being able to go with Sebastian, for being too scared to climb down, for coming here in the first place, for believing, for trying to let go of reality. This was her reality. She had leukemia. Leukemia, that was her reality. And it was stupid for her to believe in anything else. With that she fell backwards onto the hard boards of the scaffolding, her arms and legs stretched out. She closed her eyes. What had she been thinking all of these days ago? She was to go home tomorrow and nothing had changed. Nothing. She would go back into the hospital next week. Four days of needles, doctors, nurses, peeing in a cup, hard toilet paper. She had to remember to tell Mom to bring the Charmin. She could barely stand the thought of another hospital trip. And the thing was, there was no end in sight. Who knew for sure when she'd be done with the doctors, nurses, more tests, no friends? No one.

And what if it came back again? She was bound and determined that she was not going to get her hopes up this time. They told her it would be over in two and a half years last time and she believed them. But not this time. They lied. They're liars. They weren't going to make her believe again. She repeated to herself over and over again, "I won't. I won't believe." Leukemia, was all she believed in. No one, not even Sebastian, was going to make her believe she could be anything other than a kid with leukemia.

But where did he go? It didn't matter. He was nowhere. He

was nothing. "I'm nothing," she said to herself. "I'm nowhere, but, here, stranded on this stupid scaffolding. I don't believe in anything. I won't!"

And with that, she opened her sunken, ringed eyes wide. She stared up at the fake sky. Fake, but beautiful all the same, she thought. Her eyes were glassed over a bit, blurring her vision, making the view that much more spectacular.

*No tears. No more tears,* she thought to herself. She blinked a few times and once more, but the blurriness didn't go away. She blinked several times more and when she still couldn't see with clear eyes, she assumed this was another side effect of the chemotherapy that went along with the hair loss, nausea, lack of energy, aching joints. She wanted so desperately to be off this scaffolding, with Chelsea, having fun like they did when they were on the shooting star. It had felt as though they were soaring through space.

Through her blurry eyes, she could barely make out something in the sky. Something white and small soaring through the air. It was coming towards her. She kept blinking but she still couldn't tell what it was. Then, she noticed that the stars were getting bigger. And the planets were becoming even more vibrant. Her body felt like it was floating. When she was at the hospital just coming out of the anesthesia she sometimes felt this way. But she wasn't in the hospital now.

She looked back to find the scaffolding far beneath her. She WAS floating!! The white thing, the stars, the planets were not getting closer to her, she was the one floating towards them. She was soaring. She quickly realized that the white thing was an astronaut's uniform. And as she floated even closer, she could see Sebastian's wide grin peering out of the mirrored helmet. He waved to her and said, "I knew you could do it. I knew you'd find me." She had. She had done it!

Ella looked around and directly behind Sebastian, Jupiter was floating in space. It was glowing brightly with stripes in different hues of green and brown. It was spectacular. As she took in more of the view, she saw the other planets off in the distance, all glowing warmly, looking very inviting. Stars were twinkling on and off as far as the eye could see.

All of a sudden, a falling star shot right in between them. "Wow!!" Ella could actually feel the warmth of the light as it rocketed past her. It then slowly floated towards the ground and disappeared out of sight.

*I'm going to appreciate the night sky so much more now*, she thought to herself. She hadn't taken the time to realize just how amazing the sky was with the millions of stars, the spectacularly vibrant planets, and the gigantic moon.

"Let's go do Ella cartwheels on the moon after we explore Juniper," Sebastian suggested.

"You mean Jupiter?" Ella corrected him.

"No, I said Juniper."

"There isn't a planet named Juniper." And instantly she started to float backwards. The stars, Sebastian, and Jupiter, or Juniper, were all slowly getting further away. She was fading back towards the scaffolding. She looked at Sebastian with wide pleading eyes. "No, no, no." She'd come this far. She could not go back again. Not now. Not ever! But it was no use. She kept drifting.

Ella looked over to her left and there was a round planet covered by a forest of Juniper trees. Ella smiled to herself. She looked over to Sebastian, who was getting smaller by the moment. "Thanks, Sebastian. Juniper is really lovely."

And with that, she zoomed past Sebastian at top speed and

landed right on the leafy green planet. Sebastian grinned widely at her and took off his space uniform. Then, he joined her on Juniper. They bounced, ran, cart-wheeled (lopsided), soared, surfed, twisted, turned, and somersaulted all over the bright planet. This was like no feeling Ella had ever experience before. She soared even higher past Sebastian who was jumping up and down on his hands. She circled several bright stars. Then, she flew towards the moon and when she landed, she bounced up so high, she didn't know if she'd ever come back down. It was like a gigantic cylindrical trampoline. Sebastian soon joined in on the fun and they tried to out-bounce one another. Each one going higher and higher with every turn.

Ella decided that she could not be having any more fun than she was having right at this moment. Just then, she looked to her right and saw a beautiful silver stallion powerfully galloping towards her. The shining horse stopped suddenly when he reached her and bowed his head, as though requesting she get on his bare back. She climbed up, feeling his smooth, glistening fur with her small hands. He gracefully stood back up as gentle as could be and began walking. Ella felt absolutely magical.

Soon Sebastian landed back on the moon after being sprung so high he didn't come down for five minutes. He watched Ella and the horse curiously and said, "I didn't know there were any horses in space."

Ella simply smiled as the powerful horse's walk turned into a trot and then a gallop. It was quite effortless to remain on his back. Even when his gallop turned into a run and he jumped the craters of the moon, she could throw her hands in the air and remain completely balanced. The stallion's run turned into a sprint and he jumped up into the sky and soared around the moon. She peered down to see Sebastian below, looking very small and waved to him with both arms.

Ella and the stallion continued to glide past the planets and hurdled over the stars. "I can do anything!" she yelled feeling completely exhilarated. She was right, she could do anything. The stallion then turned into a snow white unicorn with flowers flowing from its tail and mane. Ella brushed her hand against the beautiful mane. She had never felt anything softer or more pure in all of her life. Not even the fuzzy seeds that she often blew off of the dandelions that filled her yard in the summertime.

Sebastian flew up right next to her on a dragon with orange, fuzzy hair and big, green eyes. His ears flopped over a bit, like an adorable mixed-breed puppy and long wisps of yellow hair projected out of the inside of his ears. The dragon seemed to smile and when he opened his mouth, bubbles came pouring out.

Ella laughed, then smiled brightly at Sebastian. Her unicorn now turned the color of purple with aqua polka dots and a bright pink mane and tail. The horn now glowed a vibrant green, just like Juniper. They took each other's hands and acrobatically flew through the sky, Sebastian on his fuzzy dragon and Ella on her multi-colored unicorn. As they soared hand-in-hand, fireworks of green, blue, yellow and red exploded throughout the sky.

# Chapter 10

Chelsea frantically paced next to the Shooting Star ride, desperately searching for Ella. Tears were streaming down her flushed cheeks. In the background sky, fireworks were exploding in vibrant colors of green, blue, yellow and red. An hour and a half had passed since she and Ella parted ways. They should have been back with Miles and Rebecca over a half an hour ago.

She stopped a stranger, who looked like he might be kind and helpful. "Excuse me, have you seen a nine-year-old girl about this tall." She positioned her hand up to her chest where Ella stood in comparison to Chelsea.

The man looked around. "I can see at least 30 kids right now that fit that description."

Chelsea wasn't sure what would make Ella stand out. She always just thought of her as a normal nine-year-old. Then, she remembered, she was not a normal nine-year-old girl. "Well, she doesn't have any hair. Or very little," Chelsea confessed.

"Oh, sorry," the man said, looking apologetic. "No, I haven't noticed anyone like that."

Chelsea burst into tears. She'd never been this scared before. The man looked frightened and had no idea what to do. Then, his wife approached them with a puff of blue cotton candy in her hand.

"Jack, what did you do to this poor, little girl?" she said to her husband defensively as she put her hand on Chelsea's shoulder.

"Nothing!" he said quickly.

The woman bent down to look at Chelsea in the face, who was hiding under her hands, tears pouring out between her fingers.

"Honey, what is it?" the woman asked.

"It's my…my…sister. I…I…don't kn…know…where she is!" she stammered between cries.

"Don't worry. We'll find her. Where are your parents?"

Chelsea proceeded to explain to the helpful woman how they had separated and were supposed to meet her mom and Miles in the picnic area. As Chelsea often did, she told the woman more information than she needed and it turned into quite a long story.

As Chelsea finished speaking, the woman looked even more concerned. "And your father past away? Oh you poor thing." She grabbed Chelsea into a huge hug. The man looked at them as if they were mad. This all made him very uncomfortable. He was pleased when his wife suggested that he stay there in case Ella showed up and she and Chelsea would go find a policeman and then find her mom.

As Chelsea waited in the office of the police with the nice woman, she felt a bit better with the woman's reassuring voice insisting everything would be okay. But then Rebecca frantically rushed into the office with Miles and Chelsea burst into even harder tears. She lunged at her mom, "I'm sorry. I'm so sorry. I don't know…what…where she went. I…I…couldn't find her."

Rebecca hugged her tightly and then pulled her back to get

the whole story. "How did you lose sight of her? I thought I told you to stay together."

Chelsea quickly looked away from her mother's piercing eyes and cried even harder. From Chelsea's reaction, Rebecca knew that they had not stayed together. Her grasp on Chelsea's arms tightened. "Why didn't you stay together? You know it's not safe. What were you thinking?" Rebecca let go of Chelsea and turned to the police woman standing nearby. "What are you doing to find her?"

"We have five policemen and seven security guards out looking for her. Two are stationed at the entrance, checking everyone coming in and out of the park. We've made an announcement about a lost girl with her description. It shouldn't be hard to find her because of…" she motioned to her head, "…you know."

"No, I don't know. Why aren't YOU out looking? Or you?" She motioned to another large policeman sitting at a desk. It didn't matter if the police woman had told her they had the entire SWAT team out looking for Ella, it wouldn't have been enough for Rebecca. "Where were they?" she asked the officer.

"We were-" Chelsea started, but her mom cut her off with a stare and looked to the officer for her answer.

"They were at the 'Shooting Star' and were supposed to meet back there before the fireworks started. We have four security guards in that-"

"I'm going to find her," Rebecca stated.

"It might be best if you stay…" the policewoman began, but she could see that Rebecca was not going to take her advice.

Rebecca started towards the door, but then looked back to Chelsea who looked at her with pleading red eyes. Rebecca did not give her a reassuring look. In fact, she looked at her with pure disappointment and frustration. She then looked over to the policewoman. "Could you look after these two?"

The policewoman nodded. "Of course. They'll be here when you get back."

Rebecca dashed out of the office. Miles immediately ran to Chelsea, crying into her chest.

"It's okay, Bud," she said trying to reassure him. But she had lied to him. It wasn't okay and she knew that her mother was thinking that Chelsea was totally irresponsible and she should never have trusted her. The anger that Rebecca felt toward Chelsea made her feel absolutely awful, but it was nothing compared to the fright Chelsea felt at the thought of losing her sister.

Rebecca's head was spinning. She looked from face to face, searching for any sign of her daughter. She couldn't stop the thoughts of Ella being alone somewhere, being held against her will, or being too sick to move. All of them were terrible images and she felt that she was going to explode with anger. Not at Chelsea, but at herself for allowing two young girls to go on their own, when her instinct told her to not let them go. For coming to the amusement park in the first place. For not just locking her kids up in the safety of her home where she would know where they were every, single second.

She thought she had experienced every parent's worst fear, the fear of having a child with a life-threatening disease. But at the moment, this seemed so much worse. When she was with Ella when she was sick, she could at least try to help in some little way. Hold her hand. Try to take her mind off things. Just let her know she was there for her. But the thought of Ella being all alone, she could not bare. Rebecca began searching even more frantically, tearing through crowds of people, spilling their refreshments, looking like a mad woman. She did not care. She had to get to Ella and be with her and hold her hand. She had to let her know she was there for her and tell her how much she loved her.

Rebecca stared up at the shooting star, the last place Chelsea had seen Ella. Then, she looked past it and spotted the deserted observatory. It may have been intuition, but something pulled her to it. She raced to the front door and pulled, but it wouldn't budge. Just then, a robust security guard was passing by and stepped up to her. "Ma'am, the observatory is closed for renovation. You can't go in there."

"I think my daughter's in there. She's sick and-"

"How'd she get in-"

"If I knew that, I'd be in there by now. Open this door!"

"I'll have to call for the key." As he radioed into his walkie-talkie, Rebecca hurried to the back and found the same passageway Ella and Sebastian had entered. It also wouldn't budge. She circled the entire building without being able to find an entrance. When she made her way back to the front, a supervisor was already unlocking the front door.

Rebecca hurried in front of them. The building was completely dark now, with only the "exit" signs illuminating the massive domed room in red. Rebecca's eyes searched the room, noticing all of the construction equipment, and she tripped over a bucket, the loud noise echoing throughout the room. The security guard went to a back room to turn on the lights.

She walked over to the scaffolding and looked up. Four stories high she thought she caught site of a small hand dangling from the platform. She gasped just as a policeman made his way into the room with the others.

Rebecca pointed up to the platform. "I think she's up there." Rebecca started to climb the scaffolding, but the supervisor had already gotten out the mechanical bucket that sat in a corner. He was at the controls, making his way up to the platform, as the policeman called for an ambulance on his radio.

"It's her. She has very little hair, right?" he called down to Rebecca.

"Yes, yes!" Rebecca hollered, starting to climb the scaffolding again.

Just then, Ella sat up. "Mom?" she peered down to her mother.

"Ella!!!" Rebecca exclaimed with more excitement than a stingy child on Christmas morning. "Don't move! Are you okay? The security guard is coming to get you. What happened? Don't move. Just stay there. You're all right now. Everything is going to be all right. Are you okay?"

Ella rubbed her dark eyes. "I fell asleep. I think."

The supervisor was now on the same level as Ella. He opened the gate to the bucket. "Come on, Honey. I'll take you to your mom."

Ella looked around, and then up to the sky. The stars, the planets, the moon, the unicorn, the dragon, and Sebastian were all gone. The security guard flashed the lights on and Ella could only see the domed ceiling, painted a faded black. There was no sign of any stars, planets or the moon.

"It's okay, Honey. Get in the bucket. Everything's okay," Rebecca yelled up to her, trying to also convince herself that Ella was okay.

Still looking for some sign of her adventure, Ella slowly stepped into the bucket and the supervisor lowered them down to ground level. Before they had time to step out, Rebecca had grabbed Ella tighter than ever and picked her up off the ground, lifting her out of the bucket.

"Are you all right?" Rebecca asked looking over every inch of Ella now. "Why were you up there? Tell me everything that happened."

"I," Ella started, lost for words. She couldn't tell her mom EVERYTHING. That would get Sebastian into trouble. They'd search for him, eventually find him and probably send him to an orphanage or a foster home or something. "I wanted to go up to space." She didn't know what else to say.

Rebecca was now crouched down beside Ella and looked at her strangely. "Did someone take you up there?" she asked, very seriously, certain that Ella would not go on her own.

Ella shook her head. "No. I went up by myself."

Rebecca looked at her skeptically.

"But how did you get in?" the policeman asked.

"There was a door in the back."

They all looked at one another. Surely they would have known had there been a passageway.

"But, Ella, this isn't like you. You've never done-"

"I'm really sorry. I didn't mean to scare anyone," Ella said looking to all four of them.

"You climbed up the scaffolding because you wanted to see what it was like being in space?" the policeman asked.

Ella nodded. "And it was unbelievable," she said with a smile so broad that she could not hide it.

"The observatory has been under construction for years. Nothing is working right now," said the security supervisor.

This didn't faze Ella. She wasn't going to think about what he had just said. She knew what she had done and the fun that she and Sebastian had had. And no one was going to take that away from her.

Just then, the sirens sounded outside the building and two paramedics rushed in.

"She's okay," the policeman told them as they approached.

"I'd still like to have her checked out," Rebecca stated, still not completely certain that Ella's story was true.

The paramedics placed Ella on the stretcher and took her out to the ambulance where they went over her thoroughly. Ella overheard Rebecca telling them that she had leukemia. *Like they wouldn't know already,* Ella thought. Rebecca had insisted that Ella be taken to the hospital for a complete check-up, but Ella resisted, saying she was fine and the paramedics didn't really think it was necessary, agreeing with Ella that she was just worn out.

The policeman had radioed ahead to call off the search and to let Chelsea and Miles know that Ella was safe. Rebecca thanked everyone over and over again: the paramedics, the policeman, the security guard, the supervisor, and God. She thanked God over and over that she found her little girl safe.

As they made their way back to the police office, Rebecca held onto Ella tightly not ever wanting to let her go again. She was so thrilled that they had found Ella safe-and-sound, she just couldn't be upset with her. Not right now.

Before Ella could step one foot into the police office door, Chelsea burst towards her and grabbed her tightly. She wailed with tears.

"It's okay, Chelsea. I'm okay," Ella said as she was being choked by Chelsea's tight grasp.

Miles joined into the hug as well. "Ella, you scared us."

Ella looked at Miles and said, "I'm sorry. I didn't mean to."

Then, she looked to Chelsea, whose face was read and puffy. "I'm really, really sorry," she said very earnestly.

Before Chelsea could say anything, Rebecca grabbed Ella's hand. "Come on, we need to get to bed. You need to rest."

After more thank yous, the family walked out of the police office together. Rebecca held Ella's hand on one side and Miles' on the other. Miles looked back to find Chelsea walking behind them. He stopped and waited for her, holding out his free hand.

"You're right. It's okay," he said trying to cheer her up. Chelsea grabbed his hand and the family of four walked toward the entrance of the amusement park full of emotion.

When they arrived back at the motel, there was a strange energy in the room. Everyone was so relieved that Ella was okay, they almost felt like celebrating. Yet, Rebecca still hadn't spoken to Chelsea since the police office and Chelsea felt horrible. She didn't even try to talk to her mom. She didn't know what to say.

Miles eventually fell asleep soundly in one of the beds. Rebecca was busy packing up for an early departure the next day.

When Chelsea left for the bathroom to take a shower, Ella took the opportunity to speak with her mom about Chelsea.

"Your sister shouldn't have let you go by yourself," Rebecca stated as calmly as possible when Ella brought the subject up to her.

"But I made her. Mom, you know I can be very persuasive when I want to be."

"I don't care. She should have known better."

"Mom, she didn't want me to. I wanted to go by myself so badly, I wouldn't let her say 'no'."

"If that's true, why did you want to leave Chelsea so badly? I thought you two were really getting along."

"We were. We are. I just..." Ella's words trailed off. It wouldn't be safe for her to tell her mom about Sebastian. This is not something her mom would let go. She'd tell the security and they'd take him away.

"Well, it doesn't matter. She led me to believe she was responsible and this just proves one more time that she's not," Rebecca exclaimed a little louder. They had not heard the shower turn off or paid any attention to the fact that Chelsea was now in the room, listening.

"Ella does something wrong and all you can do is hug her. All you do to me is yell at me and punish me. It's not fair," Chelsea pleaded, dripping wet.

"She is your little sister. You're supposed to take care of her. Watch out for her. When have you ever-?"

"You don't think I want to take care of her? You don't think I want to help her? I don't know what to do for her. I wish I did. If I did, I'd do it. But I don't know. I just don't-" Chelsea's sentence trailed off in her tears.

Ella ran over to console her big sister, who looked so vulnerable at this moment.

Rebecca watched her girls in a pile on the bed and teared up. She knew what Chelsea was referring to. Sometimes she needed a reminder that Ella's illness was hard on everyone. Yes, Ella had to go through the terrible physical ramifications of leukemia, but everyone was going through the emotional complications of the disease. How could Chelsea, just a child, know how to deal with all of this when Rebecca found it hard, herself, to know what to do for Ella? Of course, she felt helpless and scared. And perhaps her going off into her own little world, seemingly not having a care, was how she dealt with her emotions, by not dealing with them. It wasn't that Rebecca had not thought of this before, but she had sometimes forgotten. And with all of the concern with Ella's safety at the amusement park, she had certainly not been taking any of this into consideration.

She walked over to the girls who had now detached themselves and looked at Chelsea. "I'm sorry," she said and gave Chelsea a deep hug.

"You're not mad at me?" Chelsea asked hopefully.

"No, I'm mad at both of you for leaving each other, but we all make mistakes, and thank goodness Ella's safe."

"I'm really sorry. We'll never leave each other again," Chelsea promised.

"You're darn right you're not. I'm going to have you under lock and key."

The girls looked at each other with concerned faces.

"Don't worry, we'll try this responsibility thing again when you're 35."

"*Mom!*" the girls said in unison.

She grabbed both of them up and held on tight, never wanting to let go.

\* \* \* \*

As the others slept soundly, Ella was thinking of Sebastian and wondering if she'd ever see him again. They hadn't even been able to say a proper "good bye". The thought started to depress her. What if that was the last adventure he'd ever be able to take her on? Now that she'd experienced a truly wonderful adventure, how could she possibly turn back to her normal life? Her heart sank even further as she thought of going back into the hospital and not having Sebastian's adventures to look forward to.

She decided right then and there that she would find Sebastian in the park the next day and take him home with her. Of course, it wouldn't be quite that simple. Not only would she have to persuade her mother to take in a complete stranger, she'd have to talk her into going back to the park, so she could find him. But she assured herself that she'd find a way to go back to the park and she would prove to her mom how much she needed Sebastian and how much Sebastian needed a home, a mom, a family.

That was it. She smiled at the thought of bringing Sebastian back to her house. She knew the others would enjoy him just as much as she had. She rolled over and closed her eyes, certain that she and Sebastian would have many more adventures together.

# Chapter 11

Early the next morning the bags were packed and in the car. Rebecca found herself hugging the kids even more than usual. She was glad to be getting back home and ready to tackle anything that came their way.

They checked out of the motel and were on their way. Ella was still attempting to figure out how to persuade her mom to go back to the park. She would have to say just the right thing. They had to pass the park on their way to the interstate and it was getting closer. She'd have to think of something quick.

"Mom, I think I left my new pants at the park," she found herself blurting out.

"I wondered where those went. I didn't see you wear them once. Where would you have left them?"

"I think I left them at the gift shop."

"No, you didn't. I saw you with the bag when we left," Chelsea chimed in. "Oww!" Ella had elbowed her, hard.

"Then it must have been a ride. Can we go back? I'll just be a minute at the lost and found," said Ella eagerly.

"No, I'm sorry. We'll have to get you a pair when we get back."

"But, Mom…"

"I'm sorry, Honey. But we have to get on the road. Plus, the chances of someone handing them in are really slim," she added.

"There it goes!" Miles said excitedly. He was pointing at the entrance of the park as their car passed.

"Mom, *please!*" Ella begged. She was desperate. "Please!"

Rebecca looked back at her in the rear view mirror, certain something was wrong beyond a pair of boys pants. She assumed Ella just needed more rest. They'd had a long trip. "We aren't going back. I'm sorry."

Ella didn't know what to do or what to say. Her mother had said it so matter-of-factly. How would she ever get in touch with Sebastian again? She'd have to take a bus. That's what she'd do, get into her savings and hitchhike to the bus station, buy a ticket and get on a bus that would take her to Dreamcatchers. She'd buy two more tickets, and she and Sebastian would go back to her house. Her mom would be so happy to see her that she would not even question Sebastian living with them.

They drove in silence a few more miles, when Rebecca remembered something. "Oh, no! I forgot to pick up the photos. We were making such good time too."

She turned the van around and they drove by the entrance once again. Ella searched for any sign of Sebastian from the van's window. If she saw him, she'd just have to tell her mom that she had to stop the car or she'd jump out.

"There it goes again!" Miles said excitedly. They sped past the park, no sign of Sebastian.

The van drove into the convenience store parking lot. "I'll be right back." Rebecca said as she got out of the van and walked into store.

Chelsea looked back at Ella who had tears in her eyes. "It's him, isn't it? You want to see him again."

Ella nodded, biting her bottom lip as to not start crying. Chelsea thought for a moment and got out of the car.

"I want to go too," Miles whined from his car seat.

"No, we have to stay in here."

"Not fair," Miles huffed and crossed his arms.

Ella watched Chelsea and her mom's faces, deep conversation above the 25 cent hot dog sign plastered on the window. It looked as though Chelsea was explaining something to her mom, who looked over to the van where Ella and Miles waited. They were obviously talking about her, but what could they have been saying?

Within a few minutes, they came back to the car. Chelsea was holding the pack of photos and wearing a smile on her face.

Rebecca looked back to Ella. "We'll go back for one hour. That's it. If you don't find your friend, we're still leaving. Okay?'

Ella's frown turned into a look of complete surprise and then a broad grin. "Thank you," she bubbled to Rebecca.

"Thank Chelsea."

Chelsea was proudly smiling at Ella. "I'll go with her, Mom. I promise we won't separate."

"I appreciate that. But we'll all go."

"Yeah!!!" Miles celebrated by throwing his arms and legs in the air and waving them wildly around.

"They'd better not try to charge us. We've got one more day on our pass," Rebecca said as the family made their way to the entrance.

They stood next to the bronze statue, looking at Ella to decide where they'd find her friend. But she wasn't sure. He had pretty much just popped up every time she saw him. She never had to locate him.

They began in "Los Piratas de Cozumel." Apparently, Miles had forgotten his scare on the ride because he was all too eager to ride it again. Ella searched in every corner she could, paying close attention to the mechanical figures, but he was nowhere to be found.

Then, they hit every part of the park that Ella had ever seen him in, Kiddy Land (Miles pouted when the fire engine ride was closed for repair), Circus of Games, the carousel, the Boa Constrictor, the Log Ride, Aqua Land, and the Star Gazer Observatory, and, finally, at the entrance of the park where they had done Ella cartwheels, but there was no sign of Sebastian.

They were well over their one-hour allotted time when Rebecca quietly said, "Ella, we have to go. We have a long drive ahead of us."

"I just have to find him," Ella said, eyes searching.

"Maybe we can come back some day…"

"No! We have to find him now. You don't understand. He's all by himself. He doesn't have a family. He doesn't have anyone!" She continued to search, spinning around, looking in all directions.

Rebecca looked to Chelsea who shrugged. She then stopped Ella's spinning with her arms. "Slow down. We can probably get his address from information and you can write to him."

"He doesn't have an address."

"Is he homeless?" Rebecca asked concerned.

"Well, no, not really. He lives here…in the park."

Rebecca looked at her questioningly. "The park?"

"Yes, the park. I know it's weird, but he came here with his Grandpa and he had a heart attack or something and died. Now, Sebastian lives in the park."

"Well, then we need to tell someone."

But Ella wasn't listening. Something had caught her eye. It was the bronze statue at the entrance of the park that they'd passed many times.

"That wasn't here before," she said to no one in particular.

"Yeah, it was," Chelsea answered. "We pass it every day. It's some kid, who did something and lived a long time ago."

Ella walked up to the statue in utter confusion.

"I can't believe you never noticed it," added Chelsea.

Ella stared at the body, the face, the hair. It was definitely Sebastian positioned in his normal, hand-on-hips stance with an explorer's wide brim hat complete with a plume, a ruffled shirt, paten-leather boots and a cape. But how was this possible? Why would they dedicate a statue to Sebastian who was just a young boy who lived in an amusement park?

Ella looked closely at the wooden plaque attached to the base of the statue. "Juan Sebastián de Elcano (Explorer/Mariner) – Spanish-born navigator, who was the first to sail around the world. Here he is shown as a young boy, who took on the treacherous seas at a very young age." The description was then followed by the year he was born, "1476."

Ella stared in disbelief. It must have been a coincidence that this looked like her friend and he had the same name.

Rebecca, watched her daughter, not fully catching on to what was happening, but assuming Ella's friend either did not exist, or did exist but didn't really live in an amusement park. She gently took Ella by the shoulders and said, "Come on, Honey. It's time to go." Ella obeyed, caught in the confusion of what she had just seen.

Several minutes later, Rebecca pulled the van onto the interstate and they were on there way back home. Ella stared out the window, not sure what to think, so she decided she wasn't going to think at all.

Miles had fallen asleep and Chelsea was rummaging through the photos. She would giggle and let out an, "Ahh" every once in a while. Then, she came to a photo that really interested her.

"See you had seen if before," Chelsea exclaimed and handed a photo to Ella. When she saw it, she was stunned. It was the photo the man had taken of her and Sebastian, only instead of Sebastian being a real human standing with hands on hips, it was the statue with Ella standing next to it, arm thrown around it.

Ella was not certain what this meant, although she knew what everyone else must have been thinking. They thought Sebastian had been a figment of her imagination. This idea made her feel empty, lonely. She deeply wanted him to be real. *Sebastian is real*, she thought to herself over and over. She had seen him in the hospital way before they'd come to the park. He had taken her on the most exciting adventures. Wonderful, real adventures.

She didn't know what all of this meant and she didn't care. She just knew she was going to miss her friend desperately. And she needed him and she needed his beautiful adventures. There was no way she could turn back now.

# Chapter 12

Several months went by with Ella's all-too-normal routine of chemotherapy and four-day long hospital stays. Unfortunately, she had not seen any sign of Sebastian. At first she had wonderful thoughts of him clinging onto the roof of their van as they drove out of the amusement park parking lot that dreaded day. As they drove into their driveway and unloaded the van, he would jump onto the gutter like a spider monkey clinging to a vine and he'd climb up and into her bedroom window. He'd be waiting for her in her room when she arrived with her bag. He'd be standing with his feet apart and hand on hip, with his wide grin. But he wasn't there.

When she went into the hospital for her chemo appointments, she always had one eye on the door, half expecting him to be marching past her room. She envisioned him leading the band once again and she would rush from her hospital bed and join him, as long as he didn't mind that their parade had two band leaders. Even if he did, she could run up to the back of the parade and dive onto the back of the elephant. She'd never ridden an elephant and thought it seemed like fun. But he didn't show up.

Ella wasn't even able to muster Sebastian up in her dreams. She tried to concentrate on him right before falling asleep, but it didn't work. Try as she might, she couldn't dream any more. Sebastian was gone and she didn't know if she'd ever see him again.

The one good thing that had been happening in all of this time is that her hair was finally coming in like a normal, thick head of hair. As far as her hair went, she looked like a regular nine-year-old with short, stylish hair. She even massaged the roots hoping that might speed up the process. She'd gotten used to people staring at her bald head or her fuzzy head, but she had to admit it was nice not to notice every whisper from passersby. In those days people either went out of their way not to look or couldn't help but stare. Everyone except Sebastian, who had told her that he liked her head. A strange comment, but one that had stayed with her all of these months.

Even more time passed and Ella needed to see Sebastian more than ever. She was to have radiation soon and she was scared to death. She had no idea what to expect. Her mom tried to prepare her, but she didn't know what to expect either. And Ella could tell that it scared her mom just as much if not more than Ella. She needed Sebastian to take her on an adventure. She needed to forget. She wanted to focus on space or the sea or a safari. But the harder she tried to find him, the further it seemed he'd become. Her memories of him were becoming more and more vague. Their adventures together seemed less real. She didn't want to forget him, but it was becoming more difficult to remember.

The feared day of radiation had arrived and Sebastian was nowhere to be found. Ella had given up on him. She'd been quiet all morning as she lay on the couch waiting to go to the hospital, resigned to the fact that she'd never see Sebastian again.

Rebecca had been nervously working all morning. She asked

Ella constantly if everything was okay. Ella's usual retort was the nod of the head, with the please-stop-asking roll of the eyes.

Rebecca and Ella met with the radiologist that afternoon. Ella listened carefully, sometimes losing interest, even showing boredom with the technical talk of radiation, but Rebecca fired the questions, hoping for some reassurance that there would be no long-term effects, that this would truly be the wonder treatment that the doctors had been pressing. What would the radiation wave be touching? Could her eyes be injured? Would this affect Ella's learning abilities? What type of activities would help to keep her mind working at level?

After sufficiently answering all of Rebecca's questions, Dr. Wyna took a deep breath and looked at Ella. "There is one last thing I need to mention, Ella. You will lose your hair again. I'm sorry, but because of the location of the radiation, you will lose your hair, and you have such a beautiful head of it." He watched for Ella's reaction. Tears welled up in Rebecca's eyes as she also scrutinized Ella's facial expression, which seemed unaltered.

Rebecca ran her fingers through Ella's freshly grown hair and said, "Ella, I'm sorry we didn't discuss this first."

"It's okay, Mom," Ella shrugged. She was hopeful she could keep this hair, but she wasn't going to be stupid about it. There was no point.

Ella looked out the door just one more time, looking for a sign from Sebastian that she did not receive. She felt the lump in her throat get bigger, but would not let a tear out. She nodded her sweet little head to the doctor. Rebecca grabbed her hand and squeezed.

They followed the doctor to the fitting room, where the technicians would make Ella's facemask. This was to make sure that Ella did not move her head even the slightest bit. The unknown and newness of this particular facet of her treatment kept the two intrigued enough to keep them moving through the process. Neither of them took the time to stop and consider what this all felt like or looked like, they simply went through the motions. It was easier that way.

The mask was made of a mesh plastic that was soaked in hot water, making the material pliable, allowing it to stretch and form to Ella's every facial curvature. The technicians talked Ella through every step explaining that the material might be hot at first, but would cool down. She would be able to breathe through the holes, but not move her mouth to speak, as the cover needed to be fitted and tight enough to restrict any movement during treatment. The pinpoint of connection had to be that precise. As the white plastic was pulled around her face, her nose, chin, and ears were shaped.

"Are you okay, Ella?" the mask builders and Rebecca asked nearly every second. Ella reassured them with an "Uh huh" each time. The mummification procedure was painless to the touch, but agonizing to a parent's eyes.

After measurements were taken, the exact prototype was entered into the computer, which would ensure that Ella was treated at the exact same points with each treatment. The entire progression took only thirty minutes, but kept Rebecca on the verge of jumping with every move or word from the doctor.

Dr. Wyna was ready to begin Ella's radiation therapy the next day. The immediate start threw Rebecca. Not allowing anyone to see her true feelings of shock, she confidently confirmed that Ella would return for treatment at 12:30 the following day.

****

Chelsea looked at the clock in her fifth hour math class.

*12:30,* she thought. *They should have Ella almost ready for radiation.*

Chelsea was working harder than ever to trudge on with school, homework and normal life. But deep inside the heaviness of Ella's treatments were always there, whether anyone else knew it or not. She put up with the questions and concerns for Ella with grace. No on ever walked up to her and said, "How are you, Chelsea?" Their first questions were always about Ella and had been for the last three years. She handled it most of the time, but people tended to forget how hard this was on her.

No one knew how terrible it was to sit in school and worry about Ella. Chelsea jumped every time she would hear an ambulance outside. Her first thought was Ella. Could this be the time the sirens were for her?

She closed her eyes and sent positive thoughts Ella's way, at least she tried to make them positive. "You can do it, Ella. You are strong. Please God let this be close to the end for her."

"Chelsea, are you listening?" Her teacher was standing over her.

After hiding to wipe away an escaping tear, Chelsea looked up to Ms. Furman and smiled politely. "Sorry."

****

The actual treatment took approximately 45 seconds, the preparation only five minutes. But time slowed, the second hand on the clock got heavier and more sluggish with each step. First, the technicians would place Ella's personal mask over her head and bolt it to the metal exam table. With her head and body in place, they would then raise the table until the laser light beams met up with the blue crosses marked on both sides of her head. This line up was crucial, making sure the radiation beam touched the precise points on Ella's head. The monstrous radiation machine was set in the exact position. After the correct coordinates were positioned, the technicians and Rebecca left the room. The treatment was ready to begin.

Rebecca reluctantly left Ella, following the radiologist. The five-inch thick door, sealing off the radiation room, closed so gradually and softly, it was as if it were asking, "Are you sure you want to do this. I am giving you an out." But Rebecca knew that there really was no choice in this matter. Ultimately, she did not want to see Ella go through this, but even less, she did not want her to have to go through three more years of chemotherapy either. This would surely get rid of the leukemia in her spinal and cranial fluid.

There was some comfort in the fact that there were television monitors in the controls area, enabling Rebecca to view Ella during the entire treatment. Crossing her arms, she mentally begged for this moment's conclusion.

First the technician would push the button to radiate the left side of Ella's head. After the machine charged up, the red radiation warning light would illuminate for fifteen seconds and then turn off. The enormous robotic arm arched over Ella's head to radiate the right side of her cranium. The treatment was done. There was irony in the fact that the quickest treatment that Ella had received so far was the most powerful and potentially damaging.

"Ella, was that as easy as we said it would be? Are you okay?" The nurses initiated the first check of Ella.

Quietly, she reassured everyone in the room that she had handled everything just fine, but she kept fighting that darn lump in her throat that had been there for two days.

Rebecca grabbed Ella's tender hand and squeezed it. Needing

to hear from Ella for herself that she was okay, Rebecca whispered, "Are you okay? Really?"

"Yeah."

"We will see you the same time tomorrow, Ladies. Thank you so much for everything!" Rebecca always thanked anyone who had any part in Ella's care. After all they were all working for the same goal, to save Ella's life. There weren't enough words to express thanks for that.

When they were out of earshot, Ella looked up at her mother. Barely moving her lips she uttered, "Mom, it smelled like electricity."

Rebecca's voice portrayed that of an amazed learner. Inside her heart crumbled with the thought of it all and she wanted to get sick. "It's okay," she said reassuringly, but the truth was, she had no idea whether it was going to be okay.

****

On the second day, Rebecca grabbed her cell phone and took pictures of the preparation process and of Ella bolted to the table. She felt stronger today, strong enough to know that this was a moment she needed to face and one she needed to remember.

After the treatment was over, they sat in the car ready to pull out. Ella rested her head and sighed, "Mom, please don't show me that picture again. I look dead." Death was not something that Ella had previously spoken of. In the beginning she was too young to understand that this disease could take her life. Now she was all too aware of her possible demise.

It was true, though, the picture did depict death. Rebecca didn't like to look at the picture either, for the same reason, but she made herself observe it and keep it. It was reality and maybe some day they would both be able to view the picture.

Day after day Rebecca's rundown vehicle found its way to Ella's 12:30 radiation appointments, parking immediately outside the entrance door. At first Rebecca just viewed this as a nice perk. By the end of the first week of treatments, she realized this priority parking was a necessity, as Ella showed more signs of fatigue. With each day, the drive into town was marked by little conversation. Ella was usually in the horizontal position, barely able to hold her head up for long periods of time. Getting out of the car, opening the hospital entrance door, and approaching the waiting area became more of an undertaking that took longer and longer. By the final four treatments, Ella's feet were sweeping the floor, walking to the radiation room.

Each day Rebecca would recite the countdown to boost Ella's, or maybe even her own, morale, all the while hoping that Ella would be able to withstand the last few radiation treatments.

Each session would begin with the effervescent radiation administers offering Ella a blanket, hoping to comfort her in some way. Each day Ella's response was the same, "No thanks, I'm fine." This was not because Ella was fine or warm enough. Truly, Ella just wanted this process to be done. The less preparation, the quicker she could complete these daunting events.

Finally the last two treatments were here. Although the process itself was quick, Ella found herself searching for another place to be. She was tired. Her body was struggling to get into position, her mind was struggling to function. She wanted this to be over and for the stupid lump in her throat to go away. She found herself searching even more desperately for Sebastian. She knew it was probably useless, but she could not help herself.

She felt the need to scan the room looking for him, but the perfectly formed mask tightly anchored her head. What was she thinking anyway? Why was she hoping? Sebastian hadn't turned up since the park, why would he turn up now? She closed her eyes feeling her lashes swipe the plastic of the mask. *Please come, Sebastian, please come,* she repeated in her head over and over again. Just this once.

Before she could think any more her mom and the nurses were back in the room and the lights flashed back on. This treatment was over. Until tomorrow, she thought.

The next day, Ella shut her eyes as the technicians placed the mask on her head. She didn't like the feeling of her lashes touching that plastic anyway. She drowned out her mother's random nervous talk. She heard the humming of the huge machine as it positioned itself. It was unbearable. She closed her eyes more tightly and with a flash she saw him. Sebastian was smiling back to her, as though he were right in front of her. He soothed her for a moment, his reassuring smile, his warmth. She had forgotten where she was for a moment, but within seconds, the procedure was over, the lights were flashed on and Sebastian vanished. She opened her eyes to see the nurses and Rebecca hurrying to her. "It's over. We're done. No more of this. Well, no more radiation," her mom said as she took her hand.

Ella could not look at her mom. She could not respond. She stared off, too tired to do anything else. Then, she closed her eyes again, needing Sebastian to come back. That is all she wanted right now.

# Chapter 13

Two weeks later the aftermath of her radiation storm hit out of nowhere. Ella's hair fell out with no effort on her part at all. If she had a shirt on it was lined with her one-inch long brown strands. Her pillows had to be cleaned every morning for the sleep time remnants. Within three days, the doctor's prediction had become a harsh reality. Ella was completely bald with the exception of a Mohawk-like strip down the middle of her head. Two days later that had to be shaven to keep everyone from breaking their necks to get a glance at the radiation induced hair-do. Apparently she wasn't quite as used to the stares as she thought she was.

Not only could Ella's hair loss tell her physical story, the "bookmark" in her treatments schedule, but her energy level told the tale as well. Although the radiation had been completed two weeks prior, Ella did not seem to be bouncing back as she eventually did after each type of chemotherapy. She struggled to hold her head up at the dinner table, sometimes resorting to eating while lying on the couch.

Although Ella's body didn't want to do what it was supposed to do, Ella's mind wanted to keep moving. Seeing Sebastian for that brief flash during her final radiation treatment rejuvenated her adventurous feelings. One part of her mind was telling her to lie down and take it easy, while the other part of her, a part she had not recognized for some time, told her to keep moving. Live life. That part of her mind pushed Ella to get out of bed every morning, to keep a smile on her face, although it was a struggle, to even try and attend school as much as possible.

Rebecca tried to keep Ella down. She was so frightened that Ella's actual physical state was less than that of her mind's eye. She wanted Ella to rest as much as possible, making sure she was not subjected to any germs while her blood counts were low.

Ella just would not let her mother's worrying keep her down. Yes, she physically felt like curling up in a ball and letting the world go by, but her mind urged her on. She woke up every morning with the intentions of going to school for as long as she could. Some days she made it as early as 8:30, other days the clock had spun to the afternoon before she had passed the academic threshold. Most importantly, Ella felt alive.

After one full week and hours at school, Friday had finally come. Ella had pushed herself. She was ready for a break, ready to sleep in late, ready to let her body win over her mind's blindfolding. She felt her body begging for rest. The weekend would be the best thing for her now; she needed it to fuel up on energy for the next week.

Saturday morning came quickly, or at least Ella felt like it had. She rolled over and blinked the glaze from her eyes, trying to focus on her clock. That could not be right, it said 12:30, but it was light out. She slowly turned toward her window. He body was stiff and sore. The light from her window told her that it truly was the afternoon. She had not slept that late in months. As Ella woke up a bit more she became aware of how she felt. He body was boiling hot and achy. Knowing her body well by now, she realized that this was not her "normal" after radiation feeling. She was getting sick.

Trying to obtain the energy to get up, Ella rested in the same position for several more minutes. Hoping that a few more minutes in bed would make a difference, Ella lay quietly concentrating on being well. She hoped that she could beg her body to be sound. Because her blood counts were low, Ella knew she would be in for a hospital stay if she kept this fever she felt rising. As time passed she could tell her temperature was increasing. Begging her body to be healthy, Ella closed her eyes. She heard footsteps approaching her room. Her mother was on her way to check on her. Ella's book of life was about to open to a chapter that she did not like, the one entitled "hospital stay."

Rebecca's car nearly drove itself to the hospital. It surely knew the way. On the twenty-minute drive, Ella became more quiet and limp. Her fever was getting worse by the minute. Rebecca poked the thermometer into Ella's mouth one more time, 105 degrees. Rebecca sped up a bit, holding her breath.

She carried Ella's limp body through the Children's Hospital doors. Because she had called Dr. Sandt on the drive, everyone at the front desk was expecting the scene just as it was. Instead of the usual smiling salutations, the security guard offered a wheel chair. In place of the small talk while signatures were asked for, the receptionist held the clipboard and walked briskly next to Rebecca while she signed the admitting papers with an X. In place of the warm wishes for a short stay, there were somber stares.

Short or long stay? That was usually the question in Rebecca's and Ella's minds. Not this time. A longer stay might mean a more successful stay.

The nursing staff had all been prepped for Ella's arrival. As

Rebecca rounded the corner of the fifth floor from the elevators she noted the change in her comrades' faces as Ella came into their view. Everyone was always thrilled to see Ella and her family come to the floor. Although they were bitter-sweet visits, Ella was their favorite patient. The staff fought over who got to care for Ella, as she did exactly what she was asked to do, without complaint.

Today's approach to the nurses' station felt quite different. In place of the usual hugging greetings were looks of concerns and an urgency to get Ella into her room.

"Mom, let me lay down, please. I need to lay down." Ella was more limp and lifeless than ever. Looking into the nurses' faces, Rebecca could read that Ella was in trouble. Forgoing all of the usual small talk, the solemn caretakers got right to their work. They all rushed to get Ella to her room. They immediately pulled the stiffly sanitized sheets back on her bed and began to move her to a prone position. Ella began to moan. With lips barely moving, breath shoving the words out, she uttered, "Please don't move me. Please, please, that hurts."

"Ella, you will feel better as soon as we get you into bed."

On the count of three Rebecca and three nurses gently moved Ella to a resting position in room 525, the corner, quiet room.

Ella whimpered again telling her mother in a quiet murmur that she was going to get sick again. A nurse ran for a bucket to catch Ella sickness. The vomit had long since turned a green color, now even lined with hints of red. There was no substance left for Ella to offer. Rebecca looked at the nurse with questioning eyes.

"It's blood from her stomach lining. We will send it off to be tested."

"Please, turn off the lights, they hurt. My head and body hurt so bad," Ella exasperated as she slumped back to her bed.

The room was darkened. Rebecca would do anything to make

her daughter more comfortable. She looked up at the dark ceiling, silently begging God for help. "Please don't take her now, I'm not ready. Please help her through this one."

The crew got busy accessing Ella's port, starting fluids, and taking her vital signs. After the blood pressure was documented, the vibrantly dressed nurse walked briskly out the door. Within seconds she returned with an oxygen mask and monitor chords. "Her blood pressure is unusually low, as is her oxygen intake. We are going to keep her hooked up to vital monitors and oxygen."

Rebecca's ears began to ring, her skin to tingle. She heard what the nurse was saying but the processing of the meaning of it all was very slow. She focused as hard as she could to the explanations, but it was as if someone had pushed a slow motion button. As her ears rang louder and the muffled voice of the nurse became quieter and slower, Rebecca sat down, trying to bring herself back to reality. She had to focus, to help her daughter, but it was all too much. What was happening?

Reality snapped in quickly as Ella began to cry out in pain. "Mom, help me that hurts!!! Why does it hurt so badly! Oh, stop the pain, please!!!!"

Rebecca begged the nurse with her eyes. When she saw no answers there, she grabbed the phone to call Ella's oncology nurse. "Get Dr. Sandt up here right now!!!! Something is wrong, very wrong!"

Within two minutes, Dr. Sandt was in Ella's room. Within two seconds, he had ordered morphine to sooth Ella's pain. The medication could not come to the room quickly enough, as Ella's shrill screams cut through the serene hallways, bounced off the room walls and rang in everyone's ears.

Rebecca lost patience with the nursing staff for the fist time. Hearing her daughter's continuous cries for help triggered something that Rebecca had not needed to be before now. "Someone get that morphine in here right now, and I mean NOW!" Rebecca screamed over the top of Ella's cries.

The snail's pace of time caused the seconds to feel like hours. A fourth nurse ran into the room and handed the morphine to the charge nurse. The morphine was pushed into Ella's IV, and Ella relaxed. The whole room relaxed. Everyone stood like still but limp noodles, as the echo from the screams drifted out the door. A heavy silence now engulfed the room.

As Rebecca knew she would do, she broke the silence with deep apologetic words. "I am so sorry that I yelled at you all, but I can't stand for her to be in this much pain." Tears streamed down Rebecca's face as she begged for forgiveness.

"We completely understand. We felt like screaming for the medicine to get here too," and they hugged, just as good friends would do after going through something messy and difficult.

Rebecca stood outside of Ella's hospital room with Dr. Sandt, his nurses and two other doctors. "What caused this? What happened?" she asked frantically.

Dr. Sandt answered her in his calm, factual voice. "Ella has a serious infection, a gram negative blood infection. She has gone into shock due to the impact it has had on her body. At this point we are doing everything we can. She will have round the clock intravenous antibiotics. We will keep her as comfortable as possible with anti nausea medicines and other medications to keep her resting. She is too sick to be awake and aware."

"She just got over the effects of the radiation and now this?"

"We're going to monitor her closely. I promise." He laid his hand on Rebecca's shoulder and gave it a squeeze. It didn't reassure her. She looked into the room at Ella who lay in her bed, sleeping, entangled with monitor chords, oxygen tubing and antibiotics flowing to her port.

Rebecca stayed with Ella for the several days she was in the hospital. She didn't leave her side for a moment. Ella slept most of the time due to the high dose of morphine the doctors were administering. The pain was just too much for her. On several occasions, she woke up screaming in agony. Rebecca could not bear to see her sweet daughter in this state for one more moment. She hated the idea of her daughter taking morphine, but at this point would have done just about anything to stop the pain.

Rebecca only left the room for moments at a time, to use the restroom, check on blood counts, and talk with the nurses. Each time she did she noticed different patients leaving the hospital, ready for the outside world.

Watching a three-year-old boy being discharged, Rebecca felt a hint of jealousy. *Everyone is smiling*, she thought, *what could there be to smile about?* As quickly as that thought filtered into her brain, it seeped out. Ella was always so appreciative of her own health compared to other patients.

Rebecca watched a young girl being pulled in a wagon, as she was too weak to walk. Suddenly, a scene popped into Rebecca's memory. A few months ago Ella was being released from a shorter stay at St. Vincent's. As they loaded the car Ella had mentioned how fortunate she was. She had not lost the use of her legs, she had not lost her ability to learn, and she was not without any limbs. She felt lucky. Like a flash, Rebecca was back to reality, pleased to be watching the patient heading for the elevators to freedom.

Six days had passed. The drone of the hospital monitors filled the air. They seemed to hypnotize Rebecca who sat next to Ella's bed. Painted with worry, Rebecca's face did not move or change in emotion as she watched the monitors. She had drunk all of the caffeine she could, read all of the books she cared to, and taken calls from more people than she had wanted. She had no answers, just as the doctors had no answers. It was all a waiting game. The infection that Ella had gotten was too much for her this time. The oxygen was set at a constant hum. Singing its own song, the rhythmic beeps of the heart monitor fluctuated. The IV pump kept time, counting down the units of medication, giving the helpless nine-year-old the only ammunition the doctors could provide.

The interns came into the room and startled Rebecca. The paper told the story. The neutraphils were not coming up at all. She just was not able to fight off this infection she had gotten.

From her hospital bed, Ella's eyes slowly opened. Blinking, trying to remember where she was, Ella focused on her mother sitting in the same chair that was always in the room, cradling her head in her hands with worry. Ella closed her eyes to the scene, not able to take it. She had caused her family so much pain.

She slowly rolled her head to the opposite side of the room facing her monitors. She caught sight of the small, white light on top of the monitor. The same light that had interrupted so many of her adventures. She stared for a long time, and slowly her face brightened. It was Sebastian who appeared, illuminated by a white glow behind him. Ella looked back to her worried mom and wished she could do something to make her feel better, feel like Ella did right at this moment. She looked back to Sebastian who smiled as widely as he always did.

Ella felt her weightless frame rise up out of bed, feeling as though she were not in her old beaten up body. She leaned toward Sebastian. Dressed in vividly colored sailor garb, he reminded her of the first time she spotted him, marching happily through the hospital, leading a make-believe parade. He had his usual join-me grin on his face. His hands were settled on his hips, his stance wide, and then he reached out to Ella. She longed to reach for his hand, accepting Sebastian's invitation. After all wasn't he the one that had made her feel so free and at ease in the past? Wasn't that the way she wanted to feel right now?

Yes, this was the way. This was the way to make her mother stop worrying. She wouldn't have to camp out in hospitals any more. This would help her brother and sister be reunited with their mom all of the time. This would put an end to the upheaval.

She reached out and touched Sebastian's hand. Cool, relaxed, and comfortable was the only way she could describe the feeling she was having now. It was the best feeling she had experienced since being in the ocean with the blue whale and flying through space with Sebastian. It was the best feeling she'd had in months.

With a startle, Rebecca's head raised up out of her hands. The monitors began to beep, but this time it was one long signal.

"Mom, everything is going to be just fine."

# Chapter 14

The continued buzzing of the monitor's woke Rebecca from her trance. Nurses came storming to find Ella wide eyed and reaching out into the air.

"What's going on, Rebecca? We heard the warning signals going off at the nurses' station."

As they searched to take Ella's vitals, they found the chords detached from her body. The buzzing continued, but not due to an emergency or medical arrests. Ella's sudden movements had caused the heart monitor to come off and lose its reading. Ella rolled over to her mother and reached for her hand.

"Mom, everything's alright."

Rebecca slowly reached out for Ella's offering. The surreal moment continued for her, as she squeezed her daughter's hand in disbelief.

This little girl that had been so lifeless for so many days now looked full of life. She was moving, speaking, telling her mom that everything was going to be alright. Rebecca had not seen this look, this happiness, on her face since the amusement park.

As Ella looked at Rebecca with those bright eyes, and that wide grin, how could Rebecca believe anything else other than what her daughter stated? Everything was going to be all right.

# Chapter 15

Through the darkness, Ella appeared, so peaceful, so beautiful, so graceful. She had a full head of long, thick bronze hair with tiny, colorful flowers crowning her head. Her skin shimmered under the water, looking as healthy as could be.

She floated in what seemed like mid-air. She let out a gulp of air that came bubbling out of her plump lips. She was floating in water and as she started to swim off, her shimmering tail flapped back and forth. She was a beautiful mermaid with glistening seafoam and blue scales. She gracefully swam through the blue sea, vibrant schools of fish swimming with her. Soon, a merman appeared with dark curls. It was Sebastian and he looked just as beautiful as Ella. They swam side-by-side, drifting in and out of the schools of fish.

Then, Ella spotted something in the distance. A large, blue dolphin with smooth, soft skin. She pointed to it and Sebastian acknowledged that he too saw it and swam ahead of her. Soon, she darted up and soared up to the surface where she found Sebastian riding the graceful dolphin. They skimmed the sea, went under the water and cut through the surface shooting out of the sea, flipping around. Sebastian and the dolphin glided out of sight.

Ella watched them with a wide smile. She soon eyed something that really intrigued her. A rush of water was swiftly moving towards her. When it reached Ella, the blue whale surfaced with its wide smile, the same whale Ella had come face to face with at the aquarium. They soon came head to head, Ella held his massive head in her hands. They smiled widely at each other, now two dear friends. She flipped herself onto his back and he instantly took off. They flew even faster than Sebastian and the dolphin, gliding in and out of the water. They shot out of the water and dove back under the sea, swimming happily away.

Rebecca was cutting into the roast she had just taken out of the oven. She yelled out the doorway, "Time for supper!!"

Miles came bounding out of nowhere, directly past his mom and to his marked spot at the table. He chanted, "I want food. I want food."

Chelsea then strutted by her mom with iPod in her ears and she was singing off key. "Oh, Chels, you have to do…" She took one of Chelsea's earphones out, realizing she couldn't hear a thing. "You have to do your math homework after supper."

"I already did it. And I studied my vocabulary words," she said as she started filling Miles' plate with roast, potatoes and green beans all the while, still singing.

"I don't like green beans," Miles said slyly.

"Yes, you do," Rebecca and Chelsea chimed in unison. Rebecca looked at her proudly and patted her on the back.

Rebecca made her way to the foot of the stares. "Ella, time for dinner!" She started to turn back towards the kitchen, but heard a loud "splash" from Ella's room. Rebecca called up questionably, "Ella?"

Ella swam through the blue sea, up towards the light. She broke through the surface and pulled herself up out of the water and onto the side of her bed. The bed had turned into a portal to the sea and was so deep, the bottom wasn't visible. Fish swam around the surface and the whale poked his large nose out. She stepped off the bed sans her mermaid tail, and onto her carpeted floor, soaking wet.

"I'll be back. Don't worry." She grabbed a towel from her dresser and dried off. She looked back towards her bed and said, "OK, Sebastian. Don't get too tired out. I'll be back after supper." She closed the door to her room.

"Ella, supper!" her mom called again from the kitchen.

"I'm coming!!" Ella yelled as she made her way down the stairs. She now looked like her normal self. Peach fuzz for hair, pale skin that had looked so mystical under the water, now looked translucent. The contrasting circles reappeared around her deep set eyes. But yet she was different. More full of life, happier. More like a carefree, self-assured kid.

As she hopped down step-by-step, the sound of water sloshing could be heard resonating down into the kitchen. Chelsea and Rebecca looked at each other with questioning expressions.

"I'd sure like to know what she does up there," said Chelsea. Her mom nodded in agreement.

Then, a still wet Ella walked into the kitchen. "I'm starved!"

Chelsea and Rebecca stared at Ella. They then looked at each other again with even more confusion on their faces.

Miles was busy eating his green beans but said very nonchalantly to Ella, "Did you go swimming?"

Ella nodded as she dug into her meal. "I was whale riding," she said with a wide smile. "Tomorrow I'm going on a safari."

"Cool!" Miles exclaimed. Chelsea and Rebecca shrugged. And Ella wolfed down her meal with a huge grin on her face.

# About the Author

Elizabeth Gregurich has a Masters Degree in Reading and Literacy and has been teaching 6th grade for over 22 years. She resides in Chatham, Illinois with her husband and four children. Elizabeth was inspired to write this story while helping one of her daughters battle Leukemia for 5 years before going into remission in 2008.

Stacey Hendricks has a Masters Degree in Screenwriting and has been creating works of fiction for over 15 years. She collaborated on this story with her sister, Elizabeth, after seeing what her niece had to go through during her experience with Leukemia. Stacey lives in Portland, Oregon with her husband and two children who continue to inspire her.

CPSIA information can be obtained at www.ICGtesting.com
Printed in the USA
LVOW111122031111

253347LV00002B/126/P